W9-CDW-980

It's Different for a Woman

Books by Mary Jane Ward

It's Different for a Woman

A Little Night Music

The Professor's Umbrella

The Snake Pit

The Wax Apple

The Tree Has Roots

It's Different for a Woman

MARY JANE WARD

RANDOM HOUSE

NEW YORK

First Printing

 Published in New York by Random House, Inc., and simultaneously in Toronto, Canada, by Random House of Canada, Limited.

Library of Congress Catalog Card Number
52-10091

Manufactured in the United States of America

It's Different for a Woman

One

WHILE HER FRIEND relentlessly discussed salads, Sally Cutter retraced the line she had drawn through a combination of symbols on her calendar. This particular arrangement of the private, algebraic-looking shorthand meant that Patricia Smith was scheduled to appear at the Cutter house at a quarter to one today. Sally had telephoned to tell Patricia not to come, but people who called Patricia had first to listen.

Sally Bradford Cutter and Patricia Thorne Smith had been best friends so long that Sally couldn't have said how the state had originated. For the past five years Patricia had been advancing an explanation Sally felt could be accepted by only the most unobserving of newcomers to Brentwood. On her fortieth birthday, Patricia had proposed that in the future she and Sally say they became friends through Billy Bradford. Trying to be somewhat humorous, Sally had said it was hardly a suggestion that could have been made if her brother had still been alive.

Patricia had scolded her for being flippant about her poor, dead brother, and had added that she hadn't dreamed Sally would be so touchy about age. "Darling," said Patricia, "I didn't mean I think I look younger. But why should both of us be tabbed as middle-aged on account of your children? If it were the other way around, if I were the one with the old children, I certainly wouldn't talk about us being school chums. And I think it's horrible of you to say I didn't like Billy. Why, I cried for weeks. I still do. Every time I think of him . . . "

As Patricia got farther from the thirty-five she believed she looked, if that, the age difference between Billy and Sally Bradford, in the beginning not quite five years, had of course to widen. Sally's husband agreed with her when she said it was ridiculous of Patricia to think she could pass herself off as being ten years younger than she actually was. George agreed that blondes like Patricia faded early and that Sally looked a whole lot more than a month younger than her friend, but it was unwise to bank heavily on what George said. He was an agreeable husband, especially when agreeing with his wife meant disagreeing with Patricia Smith. Their feeling about Patricia had given George Cutter and Billy Bradford perhaps the only thing they had ever had in common.

Grunting acknowledgement of the difficulty of getting really good water cress, Sally studied her calendar. She wondered where her glasses were, not that she needed them. It was this steady staring that made the lines fuzzy. She had got glasses only to humor Dr. King who, in December, had again made his weary joke about time shortening the arms.

The month's squares, most of them filled with businesslike notations, blurred into what might have been a painting by

Sally's modernist sister-in-law, Helen Cutter. Helen, who had recently added psychiatry to her profession, undoubtedly would have called the calendar composition, *Portrait of a Suburban Matron.* More specifically, might Helen have said it was a portrait of a woman beset by fears of the menopause? Sally had decided the Change, which as yet had not manifested itself in any physical manner, must be responsible for the attitude she was developing toward activities like today's luncheon.

A year ago she would have informed Dr. King's receptionist that she couldn't possibly skip a luncheon in order to take advantage of the cancellation Doctor's office had received for one-thirty today. Miss Peterson, Dr. King's receptionist for many years, would have understood. Indeed, Miss Peterson would probably have been alarmed had she known that Mrs. Cutter was, for no good reason, doodling on her neat calendar. "It's nothing urgent," Sally had said when she called Miss Peterson last week, "but if you should get a cancellation . . . "

Miss Peterson said she would do what she could but that cancellations weren't coming in the way they usually did this time of year. "Practically everyone seems well enough to see Doctor," she said and then, laughing, added that she trusted Mrs. Cutter followed her. Mrs. Cutter, certainly not sick, but just as certainly determined to see Dr. King as soon as possible, followed Miss Peterson closely enough to take today's opening when it was offered.

Crossing out the luncheon, she had experienced a wild desire to cross out everything else noted on the calendar. This impulse, she knew, was a part of the condition she must report to her doctor. She wished she didn't know him quite so well. And she wondered if he was as up-to-date on hormones as he should be.

But now Patricia had paused for breath. Quickly Sally said she couldn't go to the luncheon, but that she would see her friend later on at the Alliance tea. "Oh, but she's doing that filthy book," said Patricia. "You can't miss that. How do you suppose she'll get around the dirty words?"

Suddenly hating the book reviewer whom she had previously admired, Sally said Mrs. Black would manage. "Everything that woman reviews sounds like it had been written by the same person," she said, "namely Corinne Black."

It was too absurd a comment to warrant Patricia's notice, but Patricia was a patient woman. "Do you think we'd have her if she weren't so popular?" asked Patricia. "You know she's the most expensive one around. Why, after we've paid her there's hardly anything left, but what are you going to do?"

"Give directly to the cause," said Sally, though she was thinking of the more attractive alternative of not giving at all.

This, of course, was another absurdity. Patricia said Sally knew direct fund-raising never worked. "Why, even with Mrs. Black, we still have to have door prizes. Have you forgotten it's a whole case of scotch this time? But that wasn't what I meant. I meant, what were you thinking of doing instead?" Habitually Patricia received all decisions as being open for consideration until she either upheld or reversed them. She had, for example, reversed Sally Bradford's decision to marry George Cutter, but soon had been diverted from this by the suspicion that Laura Cutter, George's younger sister, was expecting to be asked to serve as maid of honor. Preferring to devote her full energies to the more important aspects, Patricia had shifted her fire from George to Laura; but Sally had no real hope that she could alter Patricia's course this morning.

Hurriedly she spoke of millions of errands, errands she would have saved to do after the luncheon if it hadn't been for the Alliance tea. "I have to go to that. Aunt Catherine would have fits if I didn't, and you know how she is." She tried to continue about her aunt but, more often than not, her friend could tell when an ordinarily good subject was being misused.

"Look," said Patricia, "the minute I heard your voice I knew something was wrong."

It was futile, anyway, to hope to keep a visit to the North Shore's leading gynecologist a secret. All Sally could succeed in doing, if she did contrive to make Patricia get the information from another source, would be to convince her friend that cancer was suspected. "It's nothing but a routine check," she said on the off-chance that Patricia might have forgotten when Mrs. George Cutter had had her most recent check-up. "You know how it is if you don't grab a cancellation. You have to wait weeks and then you probably forget the appointment and have to start all over again."

"You never forget appointments, dear," said Patricia, "and you had your routine in December. If you'd stop this procrastinating and have the operation . . . Frankly, I've been wanting to tell you it isn't just your children that make people think you're older than I am. Of course it was so terribly premature for me, but I faced it and didn't let myself get all dragged out."

With what she felt was considerable dignity, Sally said she would face whatever she had to face if and when it was pointed out to her by Dr. King.

"That old fuddy-duddy," said Patricia. "If I'd waited for him to make up his mind, I wouldn't have my operation yet. Do you have to go to him just because he's such a friend of your father's? He sends you a bill, doesn't he?"

Sally said it was Monday morning and that she was in the midst of an enormous washing. This reminded Patricia of something else she had been wanting to say frankly. Was anybody ever going to thank Sally for this fantastic insistence on doing her own housework, for making a hag of herself before her time, for trying to save money by going to a doctor who refused to operate on people until they were practically dead? Patricia knew what would happen if Sally kept on at this rate. Just about the time she inherited the Bradford money, Sally would up and die, that was what.

And George would marry some young chit no older than his daughter. "Really," said Patricia to summarize, "you should fix your will so George's second wife can't have a nickel of that money, because it's from your people, not his. And I certainly don't know why you haven't told me you were having hot flashes."

That was when Sally had what might have been her first hot flash. In this heat she attempted to tell Patricia a few things, but Patricia wouldn't listen. Patricia said it was very silly to get hysterical about the operation.

In this area a hysterectomy was generally called the North Shore Operation. The wide popularity of the operation was given as the reason for the youthful beauty of the suburban dowagers. On her way to the doctor's office, Sally had ample time to prepare herself for a surgical verdict. Her baby, the sixteen-year-old Bradford, had gone off with the family car. How Brad had dared take the car without asking for permission was a matter his mother would take up with the young man at her earliest opportunity, but now, looking through a train window, she thought about her contemporaries who had been relieved of their reproductive paraphernalia. Was it only because of her friend's hypnotic influence that she now saw the still intact individuals as being dragged-out hags?

Recalling her four hospitalizations, she decided she wouldn't mind a fifth. Three of her hospital stays had been genuinely enjoyable; the fourth, when she was in with pneumonia, wasn't fun, but she knew from many visits to surgical patients that pleasant hospitalizations weren't necessarily just those spent in the maternity wings. Patricia, fortified by a special bed wardrobe, had had a wonderful time with her operation, and Sally saw that she herself might have an equally delightful ten days. And perhaps on almost as lavish a scale. Her mother, she knew, would insist on providing frills.

By the time her turn to enter Doctor's private office came, she'd found several bed jackets and nightgowns, in the waiting room's magazines, that she knew would appeal to her mother as being nice presents for a hospitalized daughter. And she was still thinking about lingerie when Dr. King, after what had seemed a most cursory examination, slapped her buttocks and pronounced her fit as a fiddle.

"I didn't expect a routine examination to show anything," she said as she covered her nakedness with the sheet whose psychological value was scorned by Dr. King, at any rate scorned by him when he was dealing with a patient whom he had guided through measles and chicken pox.

He had gone to the lavatory to wash his hands, but evidently he hadn't missed the special emphasis she had placed on the word "routine."

"All right," he said. "When you've got back into your clothes, come on out and tell me when I'm to operate."

Two

"I NEVER SAID ONE word about an operation," she said when she returned to the office that had been decorated by women for women. The room's only jarring, inartistic note was Doctor. Women bought his clothes and told him how to wear them, but it was no use. "How could I know about such a thing?"

"It's a question I've been asking myself about you girls for many years," said Dr. King. "But go ahead, trot out your symptoms."

He looked a good deal like a camel and many persons, Sally presently included, thought he had a camel-like disposition. He was a large-framed man and when Sally noticed how loosely his skin was draped, she recalled that many years ago he had been rather portly. When she was a little girl, her family had no other doctor. Dr. King was now a gynecologist, but through the door that opened from his private office into the hall outside of this suite, still slunk men and boys who dated back to the doctor's earlier stages.

Sally's father, C. J. Bradford, didn't in the least mind being attended by a specialist in female ailments, so long as he didn't have to thumb through magazines with the waiting women. Sally's older boy, Nick, hadn't minded, either; but Brad, the conformist of the family, would have nothing more to do with Dr. King.

George Cutter, Sally's husband, had no truck with any doctor until he thought he was dying, which was whenever he caught a cold. When this happened, George didn't care who came, so long as it was on the run. And oddly enough, Dr. King, long since too important a man to make house calls, would come running to give George Cutter an aspirin. Sally saw that these visits gave the doctor a chance to check on George's general condition, but when she said this to Dr. King he had remarked that visiting George gave him a rare opportunity to check up on himself.

Thinking of this, she studied the man who was looking at her chart. She wondered if perhaps he might have enough insight to understand what she didn't know how to express. But his questions were as routine as his examination had been, and of course among them was Patricia's. Hot flashes?

The patient said she wasn't sure. "Is there such a thing as cold ones?" she asked. "I do get terrible chills."

There was no change in his profile, and so if he'd thought the answer silly he at least had been kind enough to refrain from smiling. "Headaches?"

"Oh yes," she said, encouraged. "I do have quite a lot of headaches."

But as she might have known he would do, he asked if she was wearing her glasses for all close work. She told him she didn't need them, that half the time she didn't even know where they were.

"Get yourself some bifocals and wear them all the time," he said, "and then you'll know where they are." But he must have seen that this was a ludicrous suggestion because he didn't press it. He asked if she was sleeping well and she replied that now and then she had to take one of the pills he'd given her in December.

Now a smile altered the profile. "Then you're sleeping well," he said.

No wonder it had been so easy to get a sleeping-pill prescription out of him. He was as good as saying he'd played a trick on her, wasn't he? But before she could tell him what she thought of such a procedure, he dropped her chart and turned around to face her. "Why doesn't Brad ever come to see me any more?" he asked, as if the business of the appointment had been finished, and as if he didn't know that his waiting room was filling with women frantic to get away to the shops, the meetings, the teas.

"One of his pals saw him in the hall, the last time he came up here," said Sally. "I guess they made life miserable for him, teasing him about being pregnant."

Laughing, Dr. King pushed a box of cigarettes toward her. "Let me see. He must be nearly seventeen."

"He will be, in June."

"Mighty hot, the day he was born. Well, it won't be long now. He's planning to go away to school, isn't he?"

Had he deliberately timed this question to coincide with her lighting of a cigarette? Horrified by the way her hands trembled, Sally spoke more loudly than necessary. She said she and George believed Brad needed the experience of being away from them. Dr. King nodded, and asked if Tess had set the date for her marriage.

It was tempting to tell him what he must have suspected, that the date for Tess Cutter's marriage to Dr. John Russak, interning at the hospital where Dr. King was chief of staff, depended somewhat on Dr. King. Of course Jack Russak's dream might not be based on anything more substantial than his great ambition. Jack couldn't have been the first intern who had coveted the chance of sharing and eventually getting Dr. King's very important practice. Cautiously Sally said her daughter's plans were still indefinite.

"But I imagine she'll be leaving the nest before Brad does," said the doctor. "How's Nick doing? Does he still like New York?"

Why had he hurried through the examination if he'd felt he could give her all this time? "Oh yes," said Sally. "He's crazy about it."

"Is George working on a new book?"

"It depends on what you call new, but George is always working on a book," she said and then, thinking Dr. King might misinterpret the sharpness she'd noticed in her voice, she explained that all she objected to was her husband's apparent determination to kill himself. "Either his own writing or his editing job would be enough, but, no, he has to carry on two full-time projects."

The doctor acted as if they had finally hit on a subject worth further consideration. He asked if George's company set a mandatory retirement age. Yes, in order to get rid of the editor who had preceded George, the company had established a general rule for retirement at sixty-five. This meant that George Cutter had a little more than ten years to go.

"It's hard for me to believe he's fifty-four," said Dr. King, "but his father was the same. It's incredibly stupid to retire people like that at sixty-five, but of course George won't mind. I imagine he's got enough work lined up to last him."

George's wife said the writer had enough lined up right now to carry him through some fifty more years, and then the doctor extended his hands and ordered her to look at them. She noticed only what she had noticed about these hands before, that they were extraordinarily small for so large a man.

"Still behaving," he said as he dropped his hands back to his lap. "Funny thing, the tremor always stops the instant I enter the operating room and there seems to be a carry-over of steadiness. But there's no getting around it, I'm developing a tremor, and one of these days it's not going to oblige me by absenting itself at convenient times. I've got to quit before that day comes. I'm having cold chills, too."

To avoid looking at him, Sally fussed with her cigarette. She said there were plenty of other things he could do, he wouldn't have to stop practicing just because some day he might decide to stop operating. But he said no, he was about to close up shop. Hazel—that was Mrs. King—wouldn't let him keep on much more than another year.

Brightly, as if they were dinner partners and she was commenting on nothing more personal than his political views, Sally said he had certainly earned his retirement. Thinking him absorbed in self-pity that betrayed approaching senility, she was unprepared for his sudden shift of focus.

"Feel you've earned your retirement, Sally?" he asked, and she began to see that her status as patient hadn't been dropped along with the chart.

"Retirement?"

"Is the knowledge that you've done a good job going to be enough to carry you through to the finish?" he asked. "Many of you women reach a kind of mandatory retirement in your forties. As a rule a man doesn't get hit until he's in his sixties. When I've been talking with your George, I've wondered why I've put all my eggs in one basket. But I've wondered more about why you and a lot of other women have done the same thing. I gambled on a safer bet. None of my folks ever lived to any great age and there was a fair chance I'd pass out before I'd have to fire myself. But how did you figure you'd die the minute the last kid lit out?"

"I've got two kids very much still at home," she said, "and anyway how could I have ever had such a crazy thought? The women in my family live forever. Look at my grandmother."

"And having her to look at, you went right ahead and built your whole life around a job you must have known you'd lose when you reached middle age. Why, Sally? You're a fairly intelligent person, maybe above average."

Crossly she thanked him and crossly she informed him she wasn't the kind of mother he was trying to make her out. Her children were independent. She herself was independent. If he could see her appointment calendar, he'd think she neglected her family. It so happened, she said, that she was not the type of woman who tried to live her children's lives. Had she lifted a finger to prevent Nick from going off to New York to work? Had she pointed out to him that there were good editorial opportunities in Chicago and that it was foolish to go off to a strange city? Was it her fault that Tess and Jack hadn't got married yet? Was she trying to persuade Brad to stay at home for his college education? "I thought you knew me better than that," she said.

Without changing expression, he asked if her hat was new. And what had that to do with it? He said he couldn't say until she answered the question. "I'm sorry I've such a poor memory for headgear," he said. "Is it a new hat?"

"Why should I get a new hat for that damned tea?" She had taken another cigarette, but she wasn't going to light it until she felt calmer.

He said he'd been led to understand that getting a new hat for the Alliance spring tea, a party held long before first robin reports began to come in, was an established custom. "I thought the reason you have the tea so early is to give you girls a chance to need another new hat for Easter."

Thinking he was trying to apologize for having accused her of being a predatory mother, Sally said the veiling on her hat was new, that she'd made that much of a concession to the damned tea. But then he wanted to know if she found the Alliance tea more damnable than teas sponsored by other organizations.

"Look," she said after she had lighted her cigarette, "anything my Aunt Catherine's mixed up in is bound to be a little more unbearable than anything else."

This viewpoint, said the doctor, was one he shared. "Yes," he said, "I've had my skirmishes with Mrs. James F. Graham. You remember when she was going to run me out of business? I'll always wonder if she thought I was offering personal services. She's the only woman in all my years of experience who hasn't reacted favorably to that little gambit of mine."

But didn't he know that Mrs. Graham wasn't the only disgruntled patient who had severed relationship with him because of his reluctance to operate? It seemed, however, that Dr. King wasn't speaking of operations. He was saying there was no need for him to use the flattering approach for Sally. All Sally had to do, he said, was look into a mirror. And if she had fears for her future beauty, let her look at her mother. "You and Tess will have to go some if you're going to be better looking at sixty-five than Mimi Bradford is," he said. "And your grandmother's still a good-looking woman."

"Heavens," said Sally, "I don't care about that sort of thing."

"No reason to," he said. "Well, it took Hazel a long time to bring your aunt around to letting us stay in the state. I think maybe that was about the toughest job Hazel's ever had so far. She's handled all my public-relations problems ever since I was an intern and it's given her a full-time occupation. Poor girl, I suppose she knows her hardest job is still ahead. The prospect of full-time loafing doesn't attract me any more than the prospect of full-time party going attracts you."

"But I don't just go to parties," she said. "I go to meetings, lectures, book reviews. . . ."

"I know it's a radical suggestion," he said, "but did you ever consider doing a little reading on your own?" He had turned back to his desk and had started to write on a prescription form.

"Oh, you!" she said. "You and George are just too funny for words."

"Well, we've got to find some kind of a job for you," he said. "Something you'll be really interested in."

"What, for instance?"

"I could give you a list a yard long and right now you'd turn down every single item on it. Seems to me you have to become interested in living another forty-five years before you'll be able to decide what you want to do with those years. Now I haven't got time to argue with you. You take one of these three times a day and tell Miss Peterson I want to see you two weeks from today. In a new hat. . . . Well, you don't have to tell Miss Peterson that part of it. She already thinks I'm crazy."

Sally looked at the prescription. "What is this? Another joke on me, like those sleeping pills?"

Obliquely he said the December prescription had been for the only kind of sleeping pills he himself would consider taking. "This one's for vitamins," he said. "They can't hurt you and they might do you a little good. But they're primarily for the psychological effect. You aren't a very good liar, Sally. The pills will help if you're obliged to tell anyone why you're coming here. Say I've diagnosed dietary deficiency. And you might tell your Patricia Thorne Smith that borderline anemia prevents us from entertaining thought of immediate hysterectomy."

Sally couldn't help laughing. "She did say I should have a hysterectomy. I was thinking about it when I came in. How did you know?"

"Oh, Lord, don't be so naïve." He stood up. "The only middle-aged women who come in here without thought of hysterectomy are those who have already had the complete operation. And, by God, half the time they think we've missed part of the works. And we have, Sally. We've been doing it right along. You're right, of course, in thinking you are having the change of life. All you've missed is what we're still missing, the reason why the change should present difficulties. Why should you be bothered by a perfectly normal process? Just think a little more about why you didn't get a new hat for today."

"Would you permit a small mention of budget?"

"Only if you could look me in the eye when you said it. Oh, I'm a fool, Sally, but not quite so much of one as you've got me down for. . . . A year from now I'd be delighted to spend an entire afternoon with you, but I wish you'd get out now. A couple of Alliance big-wigs are waiting for me and Hazel's going to give me hell if they miss the tea."

Looking at their hats rather than at their faces, Sally nodded to the two Alliance members who were in the waiting room. Purple straw and lavender and white lilacs adorned one head; the other bore yellow straw wound with brown-eyed Susans. In the mirror she saw her own navy baku with small roses and violets. Even Tess had admitted it wasn't a bad hat. Why had Dr. King taken such an antipathy to it?

"It's becoming, if you wear it forward instead of hanging on the back of your head," Tess had finally said, "but you've had it such ages."

And I've had myself such ages, Sally thought, as she stepped into the parsonage. For many years she had been entering overheated houses crowded with familiar smells, sounds and persons. Why had she suddenly to be oppressed by a wish to run away, even though she had no idea where she wished to arrive at the end of the run?

Three

WHEN THE STEPS OF this folk dance brought her to the dining-room doorway, she found the entrance blocked by a back she recognized, even though she hadn't seen the pink and navy print before or the blue hat with the pink cotton-candy veiling. Identification of the back wasn't based on intimate knowledge of Mrs. King's taste in dresses and hats; the house was full of similar costumes, but perhaps from this vibrating confection came telepathic waves, or scents recognized by the subconscious. Anyway, Sally knew it was Mrs. King, and she hoped the woman wouldn't turn around.

Not long ago, groping for a name, Sally's mother said, "What's the name of that Alliance woman who talks so much?" And Sally's husband answered, "Legion." When George Cutter listened to conversation not on his own subject, he interrupted never to contribute, only to disrupt. However, it was true that the Alliance was full of women who talked as much as Mrs. King did and Sally's mother should have known you couldn't identify a person from so general a description.

From the numerous lectures she had heard on psychology,

Sally had learned that fear attended the unknown and so why should she cringe from Mrs. King or from any of the other women who differed from Mrs. King only insofar as the various husbands differed in occupation?

This was the parsonage of the Community Church of Brentwood, Illinois, a lakeside suburb some twenty miles north of Chicago's Loop. Sally had been born and reared in Brentwood, here she had married George Cutter, another Brentwood product, though one not bearing the usual trademark, and here she had lived happily ever afterward for nearly twenty-five years. Her uncle, James Fenimore Graham, was Community Church's pastor, and in the living room his wife, Aunt Catherine, was extending a limp hand. Sally, being a niece by marriage, had been allowed to put her cheek against Mrs. Graham's soft face.

"Did you ever see anything so lovely in all your born days?" asked Mrs. King without turning around. The question was put in a consulting-God voice that required no immediate mortal response, and so Sally didn't answer, though a year ago, she knew, she would have cooed like a dove.

Looking over the ruffly pink and navy shoulder, she compared the tea table with the loveliest flower-decked display in her own born-days experience. It was a comparison she had thought of before but this was the first time she had the impulse to say yes, yes, at a gangster's wake I saw floral arrangements my Aunt Catherine will never be able to equal.

Sally Bradford had asked Tony Cado, her beloved, her beau, her soon-to-be bridegroom, "Was he sick very long?" when he said it was necessary to stop off at a funeral parlor on the way into town.

Had his cousin been sick? Tony said she evidently didn't read the newspapers. Well, in those days she hadn't read any but the school paper, but if that cousin's name had been Cado, you could be sure Sally's grandmother would have spotted it. All along, Granny had said Tony looked Black Hand to her. Granny knew about the Black Hand because she had been born all knowing.

"Just because he's Italian," Sally used to scream. Her parents, although unenthusiastic about Tony, agreed it wasn't fair to conclude the boy was mixed up with bootleggers. "His people are in the importing business," said Sally, and her grandmother said you didn't have to tell her what they imported. Like as not, Granny would be cuddling a little glass of sherry when she said this; Granny had never been White Ribbon.

But during the few minutes she was in that funeral parlor, Sally Bradford began to see that her grandmother had probably guessed right. Having Granny right was the hard part; Sally welcomed a noble reason to come between Tony and his family. He had told her they didn't approve. When she asked if her willingness to turn Catholic wouldn't alter the way his family felt, he said it wasn't religion, really, it was his mother. When Sally met Mrs. Cado, she understood why he had been unable to explain. Permanent hostility was in Mrs. Cado's eyes. Trying to believe it was her frivolous dress, her slippers, her decorated hair, Sally explained she hadn't known she was coming to a place of sorrow. Mrs. Cado spoke to Tony in

Italian. She didn't say one word to Sally who knew, Tony had told her, that English was the language most commonly used in his home.

After they were back in his car, Tony said Sally was mistaken in thinking his mother had objected to her clothes. And, he said, he had been mistaken in thinking grief might soften his mother enough to make her believe it might be all right for him, an American boy, to select his own wife. "My parents aren't so wild for me to marry you, either," said Sally, but Tony wasn't listening. He said he had never worried much about his father, his mother was the one. Then he offered what he said was the only possible solution. It was a key. The theater tickets remained in his pocket.

They parked illegally where a wave of Tony's hand drew comradely greetings from policemen. The lake crashed winter waves on the ice-crusted piles and breakwaters while Tony talked and finally cried. Sally was too astounded and outraged to cry. Granny, she thought, would have been proud of her; never had virtue been more coherent about its wounds. Tony Cado might bribe the police into winking at legal and moral codes, but he couldn't buy Sally Bradford with his money, his protestations of love, his Lake Shore Drive apartment; he could stop mooning at her in Italian because she didn't know what he was saying and didn't want to know; he was a low-life, a wicked, depraved boy and she was glad she had found him out in time.

He was still crying when she got out of the car. She walked in the slush at the side of the boulevard and ruined her beautiful blue satin slippers before a cab picked her up. The driver said it was good to know there was a decent girl left in the world, he had kids of his own.

For nearly twenty-five years Sally had been Mrs. George Cutter and, until now, whenever she had thought about Tony Cado, she had recalled her renunciation with supreme satisfaction. She was a decent girl with kids of her own, but today the patting of herself on the back began to feel more like swift kicking. She was finding herself exasperated with the limitations of her memories. If Tony had turned out well, she might have been less ashamed of her thoughts, but Tony had not turned out well, unless you judged success as being based on the ability to keep out of jail. Tony Cado had kept out of jail.

When the senatorial investigating committee was playing its Chicago stand, the newspapers carried a splendid photograph of Tony Cado's right hand. He was holding a hat in front of his face. Remembering the touch of Tony's hand, Mrs. George Cutter found herself speculating upon how easily an affair could have been managed and nobody but Sally Bradford and Tony Cado the wiser. She would have liked to discuss this with someone, but she couldn't think of anyone who wouldn't have been shocked, distressed, or convinced she was engaged in a sort of crude joke. Dr. King? If she told him she was suddenly regretting that she had defended her virtue, he undoubtedly would have sent her off at once to a psychiatrist.

Mrs. King turned around to repeat her question of the day. Dutifully Sally said she had never in her born days seen anything more lovely, yes, her Aunt Catherine was a genius.

While Mrs. King enlarged upon the theme, Sally thought about how rich Tony had been, he, himself, not just his family. He had had three cars of his own, the longest raccoon coat on campus and probably the most fraternity bids any one freshman ever received. It had been fun to go with the boy nobody else could get, the boy who wasn't on an allowance, who didn't have to borrow a car or pay attention to laws. Besides being the only independently wealthy boy she'd ever gone with, Tony Cado was the only really beautiful beau Sally Bradford ever had. Not that George isn't handsome in a very manly way, she thought, as she fixed a smile for the doctor's wife.

Sally was a doctor's wife, too, but few people gave so grand a title as Doctor to a man who was neither medical nor divine but merely an editor who many years ago had got a Ph.D. for ferreting out and collating material hardly anyone gave a damn about. In certain eddies of scholastic circles, George Cutter was regarded with considerable respect, but generally Sally was given to understand she hadn't made a very good marriage. Women old enough to excuse themselves for having atrocious manners would ask if she was still living in the little house her father had given her for a wedding present. When she said yes, they complimented her on having a husband whose head hadn't been turned by his marriage. They hadn't quite got the nerve to ask directly if George was going to allow Sally to inherit the Bradford mansion and money.

For years Sally had built and defended a myth she had almost come to believe herself. Judging George by what she knew about men from the story books and the movies and her father, she had assumed she'd have trouble getting George to accept C. J. Bradford's check. C.J. had been nervous about offering it and Sally had been terrified about taking it to George. Neither she nor her father had known George Cutter very well. She talked ten minutes before she realized that George had stopped listening. When she paused, he said he hoped she didn't expect him to go house-hunting, if that was what she proposed to do with the money. "It's twenty thousand," she said. "We won't have to pay more than fifteen for a house and so I was wondering if you'd think it would be all right to put the rest into furniture." George said it was up to her.

When she went back to her father, she made quite a story of the trouble she'd had. C.J. understood that; he wouldn't have understood her not having trouble. He would have been worried, as Sally had been worried, as almost everyone in Brentwood, except Cutters, would have been worried. So Sally stood between George and Brentwood and made him out to be a man of unwavering pride, even though pride of that sort was entirely alien to George. George just didn't care about money. If Sally had taken a regular allowance from her father and reared her family on the fat of the land, that would have been all right with George. The lean she chose, to protect George's reputation, was all right with him. He didn't notice.

Only once again had she accepted another large sum from her father. That was when Nick had polio. She'd lied to C.J. then, too, had said George would insist on paying it back. Operating between C.J. and a mythical George, Sally finally permitted her straw man to regard the money, an amount George couldn't have repaid in less than ten years, as a present.

Now, looking back over the pinching years, she wondered if she had been a fool. Was that what Dr. King had meant when he refused to be serious about her budget? Had supporting his family given George what such thoroughly approved procedure was supposed to give a man?

When he was trapped into a budget discussion, George always said it was entirely up to Sally. When she asked if he really didn't care if the house was ever painted again, he said he hadn't thought about it, but if she wanted to have it painted, go ahead. She asked if the same color would be all right with him and he said yes, he thought stucco looked about as well gray as it did any other color. She'd been too floored to tell him that for fourteen years their house had been tan. Fourteen years before, they had discussed painting the house and had agreed, she'd thought, they were tired of the gray.

"I haven't seen your mother," said Mrs. King, "but of course there's such a crush."

"She had a meeting," said Sally because that was always a safe thing to say about Mimi Bradford, "but I imagine she'll come later on." This last took a little imagination, but Mimi Graham Bradford had been known to attend Alliance doings. If she remembered about the tea and came out from town early enough, Mimi might drop by to pay her somewhat feeble respects to Mrs. James Fenimore Graham. It wasn't that Mimi had no sense of family obligation, but she put first things first and her sister-in-law was not at the top of her list.

Most of the family believed the church was James's show and, now that it was well established, best conducted without their interference. But if his relatives weren't among Dr. Graham's most active supporters, those who lived around here at least belonged to his church. It was an easy one to belong to; you didn't have to profess embarrassing beliefs or to confess embarrassing sins. Even George Cutter, scion of an ardently independent line, had finally marched up front and taken his medicine. Sally recalled the time as the only one when she had seen her uncle betray signs of stage fright, but George had refrained from interrupting the service.

For years Sally had told George that joining church was the only way to get Uncle James off his neck, but, of course, after he joined, George paraded his membership as a personally discovered prescription for a long suffered headache. "Peace, it's wonderful," he told his mother when she recaptured enough of her old self to say she couldn't understand how a child of hers could join a decadent institution. George's mother, Rita Cutter, sculptor and freethinker, had slipped considerably in the past ten years, but the news of George's church affiliation had stimulated her memory of insidious poisons and deadly opiates. George's people used phrases that made strangers assume they were rip-snorting Communists, but the Professor Cutter family were simply rip-snorters. Even in her heyday, Rita couldn't have been called an anarchist, if by anarchist one meant a person willing to co-operate with other anarchists.

"Such a big party," said Mrs. King. "I thought your aunt seemed rather tired, didn't you?"

A cough and a touch that wasn't quite a shove had let Sally know that a queue was forming behind her and Mrs. King.

She said yes, her aunt did look rather tired. It was the same as saying Aunt Catherine looked as usual. Mrs. King said such heavy burdens were placed on a minister's wife. "On the wives of all professional men," she said, "but at least I'm not expected to help Doctor operate." Then, with the smiling nod of the older woman who made no bones about her seniority when it was a question of seating, she leapt for the only near vacancy in the chairs that lined the dining room.

Sally, the relative, stood properly aside to let the starving enter. The ladies who hadn't already greeted her asked how she was; everyone knew Dr. Graham's niece. One or two women breathed special compliments for Aunt Catherine, but the leisurely examination of Mrs. Graham's art was being held until the guests had got seats and the assurance that the food was still in good supply.

This feminine mania for getting to the refreshments was another thing Sally was just beginning to notice. In a polite way—they always begged pardon—the girls went for the food as if their lives depended on the nourishment they were to derive from the tiny sandwiches and cakes. Mrs. King hadn't stood here to admire the table; she had barred the way until the seat she wanted became available. Some women did think about more than food; some of them wouldn't break the decorated bread with just anyone.

It wasn't like the old times. Nowadays the church was full of new people you didn't know a thing about, people who moved out from the closer-in suburbs, or even from the city and blandly joined Community Church as if they had every right to. As of course they did, the complaining ladies hastily told Sally. They wanted her to understand they weren't criticizing her dear uncle, but they were inclined to agree with Mrs. Graham. Women had a more practical viewpoint, didn't you think, and of course a minister wasn't expected to be practical. But didn't Sally agree that these new people would be happier in a smaller church? Especially those who obviously were from such different backgrounds.

There was no official committee for it, but Sally knew the Alliance had a group of women who worked hard to steer new people to places where they would be happier than they could hope to be in Community Church. Even so, the Alliance membership had increased to the point where the annual tea put a terrible strain on the parsonage and its old-time habituées.

A woman who had had her tea lingered beside Sally to whisper that it was getting so you felt there should be a private detective upstairs with the coats. "You just know some of these people aren't on our mailing list," she said. "They read about it in the papers and then they just come, big as you please. We really should make them show invitations at the door. Where's your mother?"

"Probably stopped at the door," said Sally, and the woman laughed and said Sally was a joker just like her uncle. They both had that same delightful sense of humor, didn't they?

Was it sense of humor that helped Sally Cutter to wade deeper into this wash of synthetics?

Four

THIS AFTERNOON'S centerpiece was of spring flowers, huckleberry and heirloom silver, and no telling what might be hidden in the distinguished tureen. Aunt Catherine sometimes used crushed chicken wire; sometimes she used potatoes spiked with needles. She was particularly creative about making do with what was on hand and, being from Money, she had considerable on hand and was known to have inherited more than household effects.

Just how much more was a question that had fascinated Brentwood for thirty years. Mrs. Graham was no beauty and Dr. Graham was an attractive man noticeably responsive to beauty. That the spiritual side of his character had prevented the poor man from being practical enough didn't make people love Dr. Graham less. They felt sorry for him for having been hooked by a rich woman who evidently had no intention of sharing her wealth with her husband.

Among those who mourned Uncle James's misfortune were those who were confident that Community Church would eventually prosper because of Aunt Catherine. Mrs. Graham had not done handsomely by the new church building, but the businessmen who sat on the Board, who called themselves feet-on-the-ground Christians, believed Mrs. Graham failed to assist in the building of the new church because she intended to do handsomely by the long-needed, long-discussed new parsonage. Sitting quietly on committees dominated by men of proved acumen, Sally was astounded by the surmises that Mrs. Graham would give between fifty and seventy-five thousand, once the excitement and tag ends in connection with the church building fund had cleared away. These men were shrewd enough to see that Mrs. Graham was more likely to be attracted by a charity that would benefit Mrs. Graham, but they didn't see that Aunt Catherine wasn't going to deprive them of incentive and initiative. Perhaps you couldn't expect them to know that so publicly a good woman would no more pay for an expensive house that was to be used by others than she would buy mink for another's back.

Year after year the Board drew up letters of gratitude to send to their minister's wife. They thanked her for second-hand furniture for the Young People's Parlor, for theatrical gauze to curtain the Toddlers' Room; with their eyes on a fairyland future, they bowed and they scraped for a chance at money that had never left Boston and never would, unless civilization collapsed completely. Aunt Catherine endured the Middle West, Brentwood, the Community Church and Uncle James, and enjoyed nothing, as far as Sally could see, but ill health. And of course compliments about table settings and the way she could get a lily out of a turnip.

Admiring the vegetable wreaths that circled the sandwich

platters, Sally approached the altar, not to touch—this was no cafeteria tea—but only to get to the other side of the room where the presence of new members made a chance at a chair more likely. Today's ushers, miserably inexperienced, only got in the way.

Nobody was happy about having the Junior Alliance provide helpers for a party, but how else were you to train the girls to handle something other than Coke bottles? If the Alliance didn't want to be swallowed up by the new people, it was obliged to be very persistent about training its own daughters for future leadership.

The half-dozen Juniors who had been browbeaten into surrendering this afternoon were serving ladies who frowned now and then, but who on the whole graciously tolerated. With an arresting exception, the Juniors looked normally sullen. The exceptional girl seemed to be on the brink of tears, but perhaps it was only because she had never worn heels before. A good deal of Sally's tea had been slopped out onto the plate before it reached her, but she pretended not to see. She said how-nice and thank-you-dear so enthusiastically that she not only added to the terror-stricken girl's misery, but also attracted the attention of a guest, a young woman in black.

"Oh," said this young woman, "I thought Scootie was sitting there."

"I moved over to talk to Barb," said the young woman, also in black, on Sally's right. "Dot, I want you to tell Barb . . . "

But Dot, the one on the left, had manners even if she wasn't a Brentwoodian of long standing. "Scootie," she said, "have you and Dr. Graham's niece . . . ?"

"Cutter," said Sally.

"Heavens," said Scootie, "I've met Dr. Graham's whole family. I'm practically one of the old guard by now. Barb, have you . . . ?"

"No," said the second head to the right, "but of course I've always known Mrs. Graham by sight."

"Cutter," said Sally, not that she cared. Most of the new people called her Mrs. Graham or Mrs. Bradford, but some of them said Sally. Unaccountably she did object to being first-named by strangers even though she knew that at her age she should have been enchanted.

Sandwiches were presented by Patsy Smith. Patsy was her godchild, but Sally was recognizing the girl more by ear these days than by sight. Patsy was the one Brad so aptly called "Death Warmed Over" and so it was something of a shock when, in response to Sally's question, Patsy said she felt like death warmed over. The girl was wearing flats and a great full skirt that nearly reached her ankles. Sally wasn't too far away from having a teen-age daughter to feel some sympathy for Patricia Senior, always so chic, but she did think it was a good joke on Patricia to have a daughter who pestered the boys by calling them up all the time. At any rate, Patsy certainly pestered Brad Cutter. Perhaps Patricia Senior hadn't been quite so popular as she now said, but she hadn't had to telephone the boys.

Knowing she must have been looking from Scootie to Barb to Dot as if attending their conversation, Sally began halfway to listen. The argument was on so statistical a plane that she glanced at their hands to see if they'd got husbands. But although they were sounding like the most graduated of college graduates, each was wearing a wedding ring.

The snippets of veiling on their plain little hats reminded Sally that her daughter had advised against a large veil. Tess knew about such things. All Tess had to know, to keep her job, was how to hold still, but she looked to the time when advertisers would no longer care for her photographs. "Of course there's always the after-forty stuff and I-wear-false-teeth," she had said, "but it's a narrow field."

Tess's fiancé disapproved of working wives, but she studied fashion merchandising because she believed every woman should be equipped to support herself. When Sally agreed and added that *she* had been short-sighted, Tess was shocked. "But, Mother," she had said, "I didn't mean you! You're different."

However, Tess didn't care to have her mother too different and Sally probably should have used only a part of the new veil. But she had hated to cut into the expensive material that could be saved for other hats, other years, and pressing between sheets of waxed paper. She sometimes defied her daughter. Tess had said not to wear the print dress. She said with the flowered hat, the dress made her mother look too busy, but Tess went by metropolitan rules rather than by suburban practice. If you were not to wear gay prints and flowered hats to a spring tea held while the earth was still drab with winter, when were you to use such adornment? Never, perhaps, if you followed the criteria of the younger set who contributed no blossoms to the Alliance bouquet. Dot, Scootie and Barb were dressed as if for a common bereavement. Their little blacks had been left very basic, and they sat as if for funeral oratory or chamber music, but of course this stiff posture among the young was caused by the present popularity of the neck-bisecting pearl choker.

"Scootie's absolutely right," said Dot. "The average woman certainly does have a minimum of one affair."

Well, now, Sally hadn't known the girls were being clinical about something interesting. She began to pay real attention. The conversation, however, was more interesting in subject matter than in development, and after a while she found herself more concerned about what the young sociologists did with their cigarette ashes than with what they did with their charts, graphs and surveys. Aunt Catherine's oriental that, in Boston, had known nothing but lovingkindness was well moth-proofed before Sally had drunk her tea and eaten a small sandwich that looked like a rose and tasted nostalgically of library paste. She had decided against the nuts and cake that had lain too long in the tea bath and, being a true Brentwoodian, she did not smoke under the auspices of the church.

She waited for an opportunity to tell the three young women it had been nice to see them, but the samplings had been renewed with great vigor: one normal woman, one husband, one lover. "And one martini?" asked Sally, or thought she did. Nobody looked at her and so perhaps she hadn't spoken.

And so she gave her plate to the hovering Patsy Smith and tried to speak kindly to the girl, but she didn't want to give Patsy any false ideas. It was quite hopeless, thank heaven. Brad didn't care for any girl as yet, but when that time came for him, Patsy wouldn't be the girl. Brad would be particular.

Patsy wasn't the only one who made departure slow. Sally talked to women she hadn't already talked with, she said yes, it was a beautiful party, yes, her aunt was a genius . . . At the doorway, Patricia Smith, resplendent in a new gray and canary costume, said she had been looking high and low. What had the doctor said?

Not feeling up to the joke Dr. King had given her to pass on to Patricia, Sally talked only of dietary deficiency. Patricia said the man might as well call himself a homeopath and be done with it, but her chief attention was on the three young women across the room. She knew their names, but *who* were they?

"Experts on sex," said Sally. "They didn't seem interested in interviewing me, but they might like to ask you some questions. How many extra-marital affairs have you had, dear?"

"Don't be coarse," said Patricia. "The one in the middle looks Jewish."

"You mean the pretty one?"

"Dear, that's a form of prejudice. I keep telling you how very prejudiced you really are, but you're just like your uncle."

"No," said Sally. "Uncle James is interested in your immortal soul. I'm not, not even remotely."

"That old quack scared you, didn't he? Darling, before I forget it, I wonder if you would tell Brad, in a very friendly way, that we think Patsy's too young to go steady."

Five

FROTHING, SALLY WENT into the hall. There she could hear the music that was being scraped out in the sun room. The Alliance Trio, visibly though not audibly supplemented by a Junior who had got a harp for Christmas, was playing "Let Me Call You Sweetheart."

The crush in the living room was now centered around Dr. Graham. No parsonage tea ever thinned out before the minister had given the ladies a chance to shake his hand. Perhaps none of the other Alliance members was aware of it, and it was something Sally hadn't thought about before, but James Fenimore Graham was a man who had tremendous sex appeal. Even in this stagnant pool might be women who remembered the lost sex.

"And here's my niece in another new hat," said Uncle James when a path had been cleared for Sally.

Since he had gone entirely white and since he had got such a rotund figure, Uncle James needed only a beard and a red and white suit to make him a Santy that department stores would fight over. As she looked into the eyes that she knew were so like her own, Sally wondered what adolescent complex had made her force her mother to say again and again that they, Mimi and Sally, didn't look nearly so much like Uncle James as people said. There was nothing wrong with the Graham eyes. Of course if you had them and no professional reason to search souls, you were frequently charged with gawking when all you were doing was striving to keep awake.

Granny called them bug-eyes. She said they could see they hadn't got them from her, but contrarily enough she didn't blame the eyes on her late husband. She said the bug-eyes were from her side, the Schultz side. She spoke of a Cousin Henry Schultz who had had these very eyes. Cousin Henry had left Indiana sixty, seventy, many years ago and gone west to be scalped or burned at the stake by the Indians. Granny's stories varied but she did stick to the fact that Cousin Henry had had those purply bug-eyes.

The eyes did not protrude. Their peculiarity was a doll-like inability to hang at half mast. Sally's mother and uncle and one of her children had the eyes which must be either wide open or shut. Tess said her eyes were the same way originally but that constant practice had given her the ability to make them droop, but Sally, who as a girl had practiced drooping, was convinced that Tess was blessed with some structural difference not inherited from the fabulous Henry.

Uncle James's version of the eyes went nicely with his tan. He wasn't an outdoor man—oh, he had no objection to walking to and from a parking place, but he preferred to observe nature comfortably. In summer months his tan was partly from exposure to real sunlight, but his wife disapproved of sun bathing. Generally Dr. Graham's fine color derived from the less controversial and more dependable rays of the lamp in his study. He would have had a sun lamp in his office at the church, too, but Aunt Catherine, knowing his tendency to forget who he was when he was basking under a lamp, would not permit this.

Aunt Catherine was a far sterner Christian than Granny Graham. Perhaps Granny's natural desire was to be as mean as Aunt Catherine, but to make her dislike of her daughter-in-law bear fruit, Granny had been forced to be somewhat liberal. Sally and her brother had profited from the animosity between the two women and so had the rest of the family, even Uncle James. The existence of Community Church depended on the fact that Aunt Catherine had said, thirty years ago, that she would have fired Uncle James a whole lot sooner if she'd been his bishop.

In the beginning they had all been members of a conservative denomination. When Uncle James decided to enter the ministry, he didn't shop around, he simply went to a seminary operated by the only church he knew anything about. He hadn't got into really hot water until after he had been preaching for some years. Mimi had told Sally that the church hadn't wanted to oust Uncle James and that he had been given every opportunity to recant his heresy. Even then he had shown outstandingly desirable aptitudes for his profession. He had a magnificent voice whose whisper could reach into the shadowy recesses under the balcony; even as a young man he had had the ability to dress up a simple story so that his audience would be complimented but at the same time never confused. Of course this very insistence on clarity, Mimi had explained, contributed to his trouble. He refused to employ the theological terminology that would have permitted him to speak his mind without sharing it. His church had had no alternative, finally, but to fire the man who each Sunday was arguing against its historic laws.

For a few mad moments his relatives had thought his wife might have the kindness to divorce him but, shaking themselves out of this dream, Mimi and C. J. Bradford and Granny Graham had got busy to create what Aunt Catherine had said was impossible, another pulpit for Uncle James. To start with, Community Church wasn't much, but Dr. Graham was. It wasn't long before the relatives could sit back and watch the new church grow.

Community Church wasn't what a non-Brentwoodian expected to find in so reputedly a correct and conservative town. And this, of course, delighted Brentwood. Again and again one heard boasts about Community's free pulpit. Even people who did not belong to the church pointed to it as their contribution to the defense of freedom. People said although they didn't agree with a word that fellow said, they were proud of living in a town where he was permitted to go on, year after year, giving them hell. The members took it and came back for more. But did they change? That was what George Cutter wanted to know.

Gently Uncle James told George heaven on earth wasn't to be achieved quickly. When George asked if Uncle James's patience included the ability to wait until man had abolished himself, Uncle James said, "Yes, my boy, if that is God's Will."

George said however much Uncle James might think he'd

got away from the old-time religion, he still clung to the orthodox minister's habit of cheating in an argument.

George Cutter would not accept evidence that could not be authenticated. Until God, with credentials, told George what His will was, George Cutter wasn't going to take Uncle James's or anybody else's say-so. Sally's husband and uncle didn't get on any too well and yet she, although without evidence to prove it, knew George liked Uncle James.

There was no doubt about it, few persons—the notable exception was his wife—were insulated against Dr. Graham's charm. Sally was always telling herself that her uncle made her very tired, but while she stood with the women who ringed eagerly around the minister, she was not indifferent to the warmth that radiated from her uncle.

In this circle the trite conversation of a tea party took on arresting novelty. Hats that had previously been monstrously unbecoming began to be not bad at all, but the good time didn't last long. Mrs. Graham came over from the receiving line.

"If you haven't had your tea yet," she said, "won't you go on out to the dining room? I imagine there are plenty of chairs now."

Perhaps Aunt Catherine was crude, thought Sally as she went upstairs, but nobody could say she wasn't effective.

Six

DOWNSTAIRS THE Alliance Trio was thinly calling an Indian; upstairs the answering echo was provided by Mrs. King, startled by Sally's entrance into the bedroom. "Oh, it's just you," said the older woman. Having finished her girdle-snapping, she said she was suspecting an allergy to nylon. What would become of her if the suspicion proved to be correct? "How much can you ignore?" she asked. "I've already had to ignore my allergy to wheat, because where can you go without running into wheat? Doctor wants me to go to a psychiatrist but for heaven's sake don't tell anyone, they'd think he was crazy. He's so modern. I don't know, Sally. I can't help thinking it was better when people were either sick or crazy and none of this psychosomatic mix-up."

She went to the fur-bearing bed for a mink coat she unnecessarily said was getting along in years. "But I keep thinking each winter will be our last in this climate," she said.

Sally, digging for a topper mercifully buried under wraps the government, but not Brentwood, considered luxurious, was thinking that however average Mrs. King appeared to be, it was impossible to imagine that she might have had a minimum of one love affair—not counting Doctor, of course. It was hard enough to think of Mrs. King as being a partner in a legal affair. But, as Mimi was always saying, women had a habit of judging each other without pausing to evaluate the opposite sex. Neuter thought about the Kings forced the admission that, as far as looks went, Doctor had got the better of the bargain. From the womanly angle, though, Mrs. King was mighty lucky to have got any husband, let alone one who had turned out to be so successful as Doctor.

This was a traditionally cultivated thought in guaranteed weed-free soil and so whence the sprout that said Sally wouldn't have blamed Mrs. King if she'd made herself a chance at the alleged minimum and taken it? The three sociologists below hadn't said how a woman went about getting hold of that minimum. Sally supposed a scientific survey of Brentwood might, if the surveyor went armed with a lie detector, turn up a deviate here or there, but she was convinced the samplings would be slim. Brentwood women, as far as she could see, just didn't have time, to say nothing of a place.

"But I have hopes of getting Doctor to retire while he's still young enough to enjoy it," Mrs. King was saying. "I suppose I shouldn't mention it, but he's very much taken with Tess's young man. For pity sakes, don't tell anyone. There's such rivalry at the hospital, you've no idea! Especially in the past five or six years, since I've been making it very clear I'm wanting Doctor to quit. Retirement's a terrible thing for men; they just don't have a woman's resources. Why, Doctor won't even talk about it."

If Dr. King selected Jack Russak for the assistant who would become successor, Tess and Jack might be able to get married in about a year, Sally was thinking. Otherwise, no telling how long it would be, because Jack wasn't going to accept any help from Tess. Would he risk losing her before he would risk losing his pride and what he had assured Tess was the basis for a woman's respect for her husband? He would. He had told Tess so and Tess had told her mother. Was Jack's almost inhuman devotion to his profession what made Dr. King take to Dr. Russak? Did Dr. King have that same kind of ruthless singleness of purpose? Did surgery require a man to insulate himself against natural human impulses?

"I wouldn't be saying this," said Mrs. King, "if I didn't remember so well how it is when an older doctor doesn't take a younger one on. My mother like to have died before Doctor and I finally did get married."

"We aren't in any hurry to lose Tess," said Sally.

"The waiting's hard on everyone," said Mrs. King. "I tell you when I see a lovely young girl like Tess engaged to a medical student or intern, it's all I can do to keep from asking her if she knows what she's getting into. And I don't mean just the waiting."

Sally wondered if Mrs. King would have said more if they hadn't heard people coming. The newcomers were a Mrs. Abbott, whom Sally had known slightly for many years, and a woman obviously not of Brentwood. Brentwood minks were never so blatantly pastel, nor were Brentwood hats ever so flagrantly original.

"We were afraid we'd miss you, being so late," said Mrs.

Abbott. "We looked for you at the book-review luncheon."

Mrs. King, assuming along with Sally that Mrs. Abbott was addressing the doctor's wife, said she had skipped the review because she'd read the book. "A doctor's wife gets so used to that sort of thing—medical conventions, you know," she said. "I mean, there's no real novelty in it for us."

"I'd read the book, too," said Mrs. Abbott's companion, "but I must say I found a good deal of novelty in the review."

"Oh, Mrs. Black's a brilliant reviewer, all right," said Mrs. King. "Well, I must fly. So nice to have seen you. Be sure to get some of the mushroom puffs."

Sally could have left with Mrs. King, but she wanted to see what was under the lavender mink. And when Mrs. Abbott's friend removed her coat, she revealed a dress worth the wait. The rich purple satin was relieved only by a large diamond wren, large for wrens and large for pins. This woman, Sally knew, had either to be from California or from New York.

"Well," said the stranger when she turned to Sally, "it's taken us a long time to get together, hasn't it? Maybe it's just as well, though, because there was a time when I wanted to kill you." Her high heels and her jutting purple feathers made her seem around seven feet tall. Sally would have guessed her weight as being something well over two hundred.

It wasn't too easy to return the smile. "I think you must have me mixed up with someone else," said Sally. "I'm Sally Cutter."

"That's just it," said Mrs. Abbott. "You have hit ye old nail on the head."

"I didn't know I'd changed as much as all that," said Purple. "Of course I'm gray and a few pounds heavier."

"Few?" Mrs. Abbott laughed. She herself was very fat but, being a short woman, she probably weighed a good deal less than her friend. "May, I bet it's fifty."

"Now I'd be a sight if I weighed fifty pounds less, wouldn't I?" Purple, or May, asked Sally.

Trying to subtract fifty pounds and gray hair from this vision did no good; Sally couldn't remember ever having known anyone named May. "Well, you're tall," she said.

"Tall as George, nearly, in high heels," said Purple May. "Sally, I know you never saw me before but I did think you might recognize me from those old pictures. Ah, dreamer. You win, Midge. I've changed. Sally, I'm May Tabor, or was. My name's Johnson now. Not Swedish. Remember this when you meet Bert. It hurts him if you don't spot his English accent. His folks were born in England."

"She would have, too," said Mrs. Abbott who had lighted a cigarette even though the absence of ash trays should have informed her that smoking was prohibited in Aunt Catherine's bedroom. "Killed you, I mean. Oh, she was in a state. Don't you try to deny it, May."

"So who's denying?" asked Mrs. Johnson in an accent her Bert must have deplored. "Darling, pulling out all those C's!"

"She'd marked her linen," Mrs. Abbott explained, "even though I'd told her it just wasn't done. Well, she couldn't keep on saying there isn't usually a pretty practical reason for our conventions, could she?"

"Don't heckle her," said Mrs. Johnson. "She'll get the idea Bert and I aren't the happiest couple in the world."

"I adore Bert," said Mrs. Abbott. "Sally, he's the sweetest man that ever drew breath. You'll adore him."

"Everybody adores Bert," said Mrs. Johnson, "but I am not in the market for a trade with anybody, not even with you, Sally."

"That I should have lived to hear this," said Mrs. Abbott. "I'm going home and hang myself, I mean what's the use when nothing lasts? But nothing!"

"I suppose you know Bert's taking over the Winton Chicago plant," said Mrs. Johnson.

"No, I didn't," said Sally, nor did she know what Winton was.

"It's a tremendous promotion for him," said Mrs. Johnson, "but you know how it is with born New Yorkers."

"I can't understand it," said Mrs. Abbott, "because otherwise he's so absolutely sweet. I simply loathe New York."

"And I loathe the New York you people dream up for us when you come to visit, dear," said Mrs. Johnson, "as long as we're letting down our hair. But, Sally, speaking of hair, you might have had the decency to get a little gray. Oh, I know you're loads younger than I am, but at your age I was quite gray."

"Well, in a manner of speaking," said Mrs. Abbott.

"I'm gray, all right," said Sally, "but it doesn't show up much in my color hair."

"As my chum indicated, I dyed mine for a while," said Mrs. Johnson, "on account of Bert looking so much younger." She paused and then asked Mrs. Abbott why the sudden inhibition. "Looking so much younger perhaps on account of being," she explained, after saying it wasn't often she had to speak for Midge. "But then I decided the hell with it."

"Darling, you must watch your language," said Mrs. Abbott. "This is not New York."

"Mrs. Hemingway-Black found it heavy going for a while during her review," said Mrs. Johnson, "until she caught on to why we weren't responding every time she said *obscenity*. We tittered beautifully after she began saying *barn-obscenity* or *back-fence-obscenity*. J[illegible]s!"

"May, really!" said Mrs. Abbott. "Sally, you tell her we simply don't talk like that in Brentwood."

"I am very displeased with Brentwood at the moment," said Mrs. Johnson. "Sally, I had to pay ten thousand dollars more for a hovel in that new subdivision than I got for my beautiful house in Bronxville. And the taxes! You could rent a good apartment in Manhattan for less."

While Mrs. Johnson continued in this vein, Sally and Mrs. Abbott exchanged the midwesterner's look of complacent superiority, but suddenly the subject was changed. "How is old George, anyway?" asked Mrs. Johnson.

Sally said he was fine.

"And the children?" asked Mrs. Johnson.

"They're fine, too," said Sally.

"I wrote you about the older boy," said Mrs. Abbott. "Don't you read your mail?"

"I read your letters with difficulty, Midge, but I do read them," said Mrs. Johnson. "Sally, this transfer business came up before I could do anything about Nick. I would have had him out to the house, otherwise."

"That's very kind of you," said Sally. She looked at her watch and said she hadn't realized it was so late.

"Wait a minute," said Mrs. Johnson. "Midge, when am I going to call on the Cutters? Sally, I would have got in touch with you sooner, but I had to settle this house business. Bert's going to have apoplexy. Midge, don't keep the girl waiting. When?"

"If you mean while you're still with us, I don't know," said Mrs. Abbott.

"But when Bert and the furniture get here I'm going to be wild and I don't want to wait until that's out of the way," said Mrs. Johnson. "What's wrong with tonight?"

"The Taylors expect us nineish," said Mrs. Abbott.

"Then suppose I drop around at your place after dinner," Mrs. Johnson said to Sally.

"Eightish," said Mrs. Abbott. "That would give me an hour to rest up."

"Midge, Sally's caught on that we're best friends." Mrs. Johnson turned to ask if tonight was all right with Sally.

Sally's policy was to get the inevitable over with as soon as possible. George's was to put it off; also, George never saw there was such a thing as being cornered. She said tonight would be fine for her, but that she couldn't say for sure about George, because of a deadline. . . .

Mrs. Johnson laughed. She said it just went to show that old George hadn't changed. She said you couldn't tell her a thing about old George, she knew that rascal. "After all," she said, "we were engaged for over a year. Long engagements just never are a good idea, are they?"

If, many years ago, George had told Sally he'd once been engaged to another woman, she wouldn't have been stunned, but when the news came at this late date from a woman she had never heard of before, it buckled her knees. However, she hadn't grown up in Brentwood for nothing. She had a mask for her face and a control for her voice. "Well," she said, "you wouldn't expect me to agree in this particular case, would you?"

Seven

SHE WAS A BORN talker, but motherhood had imposed its restraints. She had had the one quiet child but hadn't known, until too late, that this should have caused her great alarm. But even in her modern wisdom it was still impossible not to look back on Nick's quietness with gratitude; two chatterboxes had seemed all this small house could contain. Now while her two born talkers handled the dinner conversation, it crossed her mind that the listening role was one she might never have to retire from.

Did George brood about the decreasing of parental duties? In his way he had been a devoted father, but George's fatherly way wasn't what Brentwood held up as the ideal. Currently a Mr. Gibson, who would leave his office to attend football and basketball practice, was cited as the town's perfect parent. Mr. Gibson was a real pal to his boy. This may have delighted Peter Gibson, but Brad Cutter had never said he wished *his* father would join the gang. Forced to give an opinion, Brad said Mr. Gibson was okay, for an old guy. The Gibson man was at least ten years younger than George Cutter, but Sally hadn't scolded Brad. She'd known what he meant. Often the gang was stuck with a younger brother who was okay for a young guy; that was life. As Brad was always saying, you had to take the bitter with the better.

Sally approved of the philosophy, but she did wish Brad would think of another way to phrase it. Though when Brad thought of other ways to phrase things . . . He was saying "Ceiling-brown's," these days, for "Walgreen's." Even George, whose taste in humor seemed to Sally to be very primitive, found some of Brad's cleverness, now called cleaverness, unpalatable.

When Sally converted herself into a listener she did a fairly good job, but George, who called himself a born listener, rarely deviated from his habitual social deafness. He made a great show of listening, but of course his children had long since seen through him. They seemed not to mind. They often made a game of proving how little Daddy heard.

Daddy sat with his head bent forward. His eyes, a dark but very alive brown, seldom strayed from the speaker. If you hadn't known him, you would have said George Cutter was hanging on every word, memorizing it, building his future around it. Sally had been married to him several weeks before she realized that behind the alert façade George roamed far and wide in space and time.

Of his children, the only one who had discovered how to hold the father's prolonged attention, or maybe the only one who wanted it, was Nicolas. During his convalescence from infantile paralysis, Nick got into the habit of writing letters to his father. Living under the same roof, the father and son had carried on a voluminous correspondence that lasted until Nick went east for his graduate work. Away from home, Nick addressed his letters to the whole family, but Sally knew he was still writing primarily to his father. And now that Nick, too, was an editor, though in a very minor way, he and his father had even more in common.

There was no physical resemblance between the two. People always said Nick was the one who should have been called Bradford. They said Nick was the spit and image of C. J. Bradford. Sally never did know what the spit referred to, but Nick, though he lacked C.J.'s neatness, was certainly his grandfather Bradford's image. Inside, however, Nick was another George. Never quite reaching George, Sally had never quite reached Nick. Because of Nick's long illness she had been with him more than she'd been with her other children but, even so, she felt she didn't know Nick very well.

Listening to Tess's account of the day's work, a story that included enough about lighting technicalities to hold Brad, Sally let part of her mind wander around the dining room. The pale green of the wallpaper's background wasn't cleaning up well any more. She had thought the pattern of climbing ivy too insipid to become tiresome, but she was tired of it. She wished someone would discuss wallpaper with her.

Brad couldn't be expected to be interested. Tess would try, but Tess couldn't help it, she was thinking about a future home rather than about the present one. George would pretend to listen and then he would say, "Whatever you think, dear." Sally's mother would listen, of course. But Mimi was so busy with important things, social service and civic welfare, that Sally hesitated to bother her with wallpaper. It was a husband's job as well as a wife's, wasn't it? But Sally's husband had never seen it that way.

He never noticed anything; he would eat anything, and he almost never raised his voice; the only disturbance he caused around home was when he forgot to close his study door. But even when the door was open, the typewriter didn't make much racket. Several of her friends who had problem husbands, men who were always sticking their noses into women's business, said Sally should thank her stars for having a man she could push around. It was true that she could push George around any old way, so long as it didn't take him out of his own way. If she told him the dining room would be more cheerful if something were done to the shiny brown woodwork, he would suggest that she do something about it. He might even recall that she had done something about the bathroom and kitchen.

But those rooms were small enough for her to cope with, and the dining room, maddeningly, was the largest in the house. There were times when she wished she could find the architect and shoot him dead, though it was unrealistic to think such a house as this could have had an architect. If the partition between the living and dining rooms had been removed, the Cutters would have had one very decent room, but where was the money for such an enterprise? Several years ago, Mr. Gibson, whom Sally was learning to hate, had taken a partition out of his house all by himself. Sally had talked about this, had told George how Mr. Gibson had never so much as hung a picture before. George said Gibson certainly was a clever fellow, but there would have been cause for real alarm if George Cutter had been inspired to take up remodeling. He couldn't even build a fire.

On the dining room's east wall were French windows that opened into a glazed cubicle too small for any useful purpose beyond providing an out-of-the-way place for seedlings. Oh, for a while it had served Brad as a passably adequate railway yard, but then that miserable Mr. Gibson had got the miniature-train bug and had made a boy's heaven of his basement. Peter Gibson, thought Sally, would come to a bad end. She was obliged to think this if she wanted to see good ends for her children. She simply could not compete with Mr. Gibson. Naturally she liked to think that Gibson's intense interest in children indicated lack of interest in Mrs. Gibson, but this was a line of reasoning that Mrs. Cutter wasn't sure she wished to explore thoroughly.

Perhaps she should pay more attention to the niceties, such as linen napkins instead of paper? As a bride she had set a card table in the sun room each morning. She had called it the breakfast room and had made breakfast a meal that featured shower and wedding-gift finery. All through her first pregnancy she was very artistic about meals, especially breakfast. She never let George know how ashamed she had been of her failure to throw up. She didn't tell him how terrified she was by her deviation from what everyone but Dr. King said was the normal. Dr. King had congratulated her upon not having the urge to reject the fetus. Of course women still refused to accept this masculine explanation of morning sickness, but it had sounded even crazier in those days than it sounded now. Sally had assumed he was trying to keep some horrid truth from her, and after a while had learned to tell the inquiring ladies that she was sick as a dog every morning.

After Nick's birth, breakfast was served in the kitchen, from stove to kitchen table to highchair, and no fancywork added to dishpan or washtub. It was during Nick's first year, the period of Sally's greatest disorganization, that George began to call this house Diaperville. The second child, being a girl, was doomed. While the grandmothers politely argued about whether they would call the baby Little Sally or Little Rita, the pun-makers were roaring delight. Sally had never yet smiled at a pun and she was not among those who obliged with groans, but she thought Tess a good solution for the name problem and in time George and his father had stopped referring to the name's origin. The Professor, who, like George, hated to let go of what he considered a good thing, let go after he had explained to Sally's grandmother why he and George had chosen the name Tess. "We always called them didies," said Granny when the Professor had finished his little joke about Tess of the Diapervilles.

"How such a birdbrain could get so far," Tess was saying now of her employer. She was so young, so beautiful that even her grimace was attractive. This wasn't only her mother's opinion; it was one held by persons who had commercial interest in beauty.

Often when she looked at her daughter, Sally marveled at how nature could rearrange and combine ingredients and produce something superior to what you would have thought impossible, considering what there'd been to do with. Tess, taller than any woman in the known history of Sally's people, had stopped growing at five-eight, something below par for the Cutters' historic females. Tess was slender, but not naturally so. At thirteen she had worn a size eighteen and, going around with other young monsters, hadn't worried about calories. At twenty-two, a professional model, Tess was a size twelve and always worried about a tendency to slide in the direction of a fatal fourteen.

Nobody but a Cutter-Cutter could have said it was anything but a blessing that Tess hadn't got Cutter features. Sally was thankful that Brad was the only one of her children so endowed; Brad had the height and sex for that nose. George and his sisters, offspring of cousins, hadn't had much chance at a more moderate design. His sisters, Helen and Laura, acted as if fate had favored rather than betrayed them and of course sporting acceptance of what you'd got was healthy, and cheaper than plastic surgery. Privately Mimi and Sally had often agreed it had been high time to introduce something new into the Cutter family.

And what might May Tabor have introduced into the Cutter line? It was necessary to prepare the family for what was coming eightish, but there was no rush, and no opportunity at the moment.

Adroitly Brad got the floor. The children really had grown up. It was no longer a case of which could outyell the other; no longer was Mother required to step in to say whose turn it was to speak. Tess and Brad had learned how to conduct competitive conversation and would get along in life in a way their older brother would never do, or want to do. Tess's description of her boss had given Brad a chance to introduce his own best example of the birdbrain species, his English teacher. That a child of his could be so stupid about words and grammar had never ceased to astound George. When Sally countered that she had never ceased to be astounded by Nick's inability to master the simplest arithmetic, George said that was an entirely different thing, not an easy point to rebut.

Was it just three years ago that the youngest illiterate—not the younger, because Sally was right in there with Tess and Brad—of this family had got his grammar-school diploma? Sally wanted to choke the teacher responsible for making Bradford Cutter march up to the stage with the tallest girl in the class. Brad's growth had been localized for a while. Such hands and feet that little boy had had! Sally suffered while her friends told her Dr. King didn't know what he was talking about, because anyone with eyes in her head could see that Brad was going to be a little man, like C. J. Bradford, like all the Bradfords. When informed of the Supreme Court decision, Dr. King said if the ladies were right, Brad would be able to earn his fortune in freak shows. The doctor's way of putting a person's mind at ease had, as he had indicated, given his wife a busy life.

But finally the rest of Brad caught up with his hands and feet and now he was six foot three, an inch under George, when George stood up straight. Let me see, thought Sally, when was that? They had both stood very straight for the wedding, to prove they didn't care if people were saying they hardly knew each other. Of course George hadn't cared, but for a wonder he had remembered his promise to act as if he did. He had been rather extreme about carrying out his instructions; during the reception he had pretended to be unable to remember Granny's name. But Granny had started it by pretending to have forgotten his name. Sally knew that more than one guest at her wedding had said this was a marriage that wouldn't last. On one side of the church, the gloomy prediction was based on money or the lack of money; on the other side, the whispering was about brains, or the lack of brains.

On the brainy side, had people muttered that George would have done better to stick to May Tabor? Why had he put Sally in the embarrassing position of having to pretend she knew what she had never heard? It wouldn't have cost him much breath to say he had been engaged before. Sally hadn't told him about Tony Cado, come to think of it, but that was different. Like English and arithmetic? But George couldn't have felt about May as Sally had felt about Tony.

Or could he have?

Eight

SERVING DESSERT, SHE caught successfully at a pause. When she said she thought someone might ask about *her* day, the children stared, Tess in feminine alarm and Brad in tolerant, offensively masculine affection. "Dear," he said, "was it one of those?" For some months now he had been converting himself into a character that only a mother could love, but perhaps none but his mother could have been so sensitive.

Sally understood why, after an excruciatingly long period of uncertainty, Brad now gloried in his dependable bass, but had he to act as if his next birthday would be his seventieth rather than his seventeenth? The comb marks in his reddish brown hair, never, even when not plastered down, so curly as George's, reminded Sally of her father. But Brad's manner was more reminiscent of her father's father. Of course when Brad was being funny, he seemed very like Professor Cutter.

It was inconsistent, after so many years of despairing over the job of getting Brad to look a little less grubby, to be comforted to notice that his new fastidiousness had not reached his fingernails, but Sally found herself consoled by those black, broken rims. Going steady indeed! The only basis Patricia had for her claim was her daughter's desire. Brad was still just a kid. His mother decided not to bring the subject of the car up in open meeting.

When the family discussed the use of the car, Tess would sound as pious as her great-grandmother. What an angelic past Tess presented for her brother's instruction! Had Tess ever gone off with the car without asking? Had Tess ever forced poor little Mother to stand on bus corners? The more Tess talked, the littler and poorer Mother became and the more selfish and hoggish became Brad. Tess would demand that Daddy back her up. Daddy would, and then just as willingly he would swing to the opposition. George would ask why Mother would stand on bus corners. What was the matter with the streetcars? Then it would be necessary to inform him again that Brentwood no longer had streetcars. This was always shocking news for George.

"That's too bad," he would say, because he had always liked streetcars, and then he would switch to bicycles. George had also always liked bicycles.

Then Brad would tell him that upperclassmen did not ride bicycles, and Tess and George would laugh. They thought it terribly funny for a junior in high school to talk about being an upperclassman. Sally knew it was hard to remember that such a tall boy was still a child and she knew Brad had to learn to take what was directed at him, but she wished his way of taking it had been more acceptable or comprehensible to his father. George hadn't forgotten how it was to be young, but what he remembered was how it was to be a young Cutter-

Cutter. He forgot that his younger son was more than Bradford in name. Brad cared about the opinions of his group and nobody could force him to flout that group's conventions. His gang had stopped riding bicycles. Brad didn't care if his grandfather Cutter had ridden a bike every day to meet his classes, Bradford Cutter wasn't going to pedal to high school. His friends didn't ride bikes any more and that was that.

But now, unable to see that his mother intended to speak to him privately about the car, Brad emerged from his sophisticated shell. "Look," he said, "you were on the phone when I left. I waited and waited, but you never quit talking and I was late already and . . . "

To prevent Tess from leaping to the attack, Sally remarked that the pudding was a little dry and that they must use plenty of cream. As she had known it would do, the mention of cream made Tess forget about poor little Mother's lack of transportation facilities. "Ye gods," said Tess, "I shouldn't even eat it without."

"You are entirely too thin," said George. It was his first contribution to the evening.

"Do you want me to lose my job?" asked Tess.

"Yes," said George.

"Go on, Mother," said Tess. "At least *I* am listening."

"Thank you, dear," said Sally, "but what I have to say should be of special interest to Daddy."

"Yes, indeed, to be sure," said George. He was always responsive to the mention of Daddy.

"This afternoon I learned that Daddy was engaged for a year or so to a woman I had never heard of before," said Sally.

"Take all the cream you want, Brad. There's more in the kitchen."

"When was all this?" asked Brad.

"This afternoon," said his sister. "If you'd listen . . ."

"Look, stupe," said Brad, "I meant when was he engaged?"

"Just last week, natch," said Tess.

"Very interesting," said George.

"Daddy," said Tess, "did you hear what Mother said?"

"No thanks, dear," said George. "No more cream."

"George," said Sally, "this afternoon I met a woman who told me she used to be engaged to you."

"What woman, dear?" asked George.

Tess and Brad burst into raucous laughter which Brad punctuated with several piercing wolf whistles. When Tess had recovered enough to speak, she asked if the woman was cute.

"That doesn't seem quite the word," said Sally, "but you can judge for yourself. She's coming to see us tonight."

George slammed a hand down flat on the table. "Sally," he said, "I do not propose to spend my evening listening to May's gabble."

"He was stalling," said Tess. "He knew who it was right away."

"Who else would it be?" asked George.

"We wouldn't know, dear," said Sally. "We came in late. Children, her name is Johnson."

"Tabor," said George.

"I hate to be the bearer of bad news," said Sally, "but she got married."

"It's queer he never mentioned it," said George. "I've corresponded with him ever since his *Man Through the Ages*, but he's never once mentioned May."

"It's a small world," said Sally. "Fancy Bert Johnson being one of your writers. No, George, I'm afraid the world isn't quite that small, or your business so lucrative."

"Every time I've written to Tom I've wanted to add regards to May," said George, "but as he'd never mentioned her, I rather hated to. Awkward situation, especially when the book didn't go."

"Yes," said Sally, "and especially when she was married to Bert Johnson. You know, to look at her I wouldn't have dreamed she'd had such an interesting past."

"Who's Bert Johnson?" asked George.

"Her husband," said Sally. "That is, if you'll take her word for it."

George looked as if he wouldn't. "But what about Tommy?" he asked.

"George, I do not know what about Tommy," said Sally. "I just know about Bertie. His parents were born in England and he's sad about coming to Chicago to head Winton, even though it's a big promotion. You know how it is with New Yorkers."

George asked what Winton was and Sally said she didn't know but that he could bet his boots it wasn't a textbook publisher. "You wait till you see her mink coat," she said. "That didn't come out of any *Man Through the Ages*."

Brad and Tess were shaking their heads. "Winton just happens to be one of the biggest soap manufacturers in the country," said Tess.

"Everybody knows that," said Brad. "They've got a whole hour on Sunday night."

"So she didn't marry Tommy after all," said George.

"All I know is that she's not married to him now," said Sally. "And she's got over wanting to kill me. Isn't it wonderful what time will do?"

"I didn't know you and May knew each other," said George. "Why didn't you ever say so?"

"Look," said Sally, "you can want to kill people without knowing them. It wasn't on account of my personality, it was on account of you."

"Old May was always a great one for a joke," said George. "That sounds like her, all right."

"It's nice you feel the same way about each other," said Sally. "I mean, she calls you old George. But you don't have to be nervous, dear. She says she doesn't want to trade."

"Damn," said Tess. "Just as I was thinking I'd get a mink coat out of the deal."

George pushed his chair back. "We'll have to get together some time," he said.

"We're getting together tonight," said Sally. "Not Bert. He hasn't come yet. She's bought a hovel in the new subdivision, you know, where the minimum for hovels is fifty thousand, and after she gets settled we're going to be as thick as all get-out."

"Well, now," said George, "I don't think you need to worry

too much about old May. She's not so bad. You tell her we'll get together some time."

"Tonight, George," said Sally. "May Tabor Johnson is calling on us tonight between eight and nine. I mean, she's coming eightish and leaving nineish."

"Oh, one of those kind," said Brad.

"*That* kind," said George.

"Well, Dad," said Brad, "I guess you ought to know."

Sally and Tess complimented Brad, but George wasn't in the mood for humor. He said he had a deadline.

"I told her," said Sally, "but she said I couldn't tell her a thing about old George."

"Well, chicks," said Brad, "this is where I came in. Mother, I'm studying at Pete's place tonight."

"Then I suppose nobody will mind if I take the car," said Tess. "I'll pick Jack up at the hospital and save him the trip."

"I hate to disappoint Mr. Gibson and Dr. Russak," said Sally, "but you two are going to be on deck. Mrs. Johnson wants to meet old George's children and it's not going to hurt you to let her look at you for a few minutes. And it won't hurt Jack to come over and see a little more of what he's getting into."

"Don't you think meeting Daddy's old fiancée is carrying it a little far?" asked Tess.

"She wasn't my fiancée," said George.

"George, a gentleman would hardly say such a thing after a woman's flatly said she was engaged to him for more than a year," said Sally.

"May was around the house a good deal," said George. "The Professor took quite a shine to her."

Tess said this was a new low. She said she would be ashamed to put it off onto someone who couldn't defend himself. "I see what you mean, Mother," she said. "Gad! I'll stay, and so will you, Master Bradford. Gad!"

George asked if Tess was making a semantic concession to Dr. Russak. He said he had a book that would give his daughter more range for her expletives, but Sally interrupted this deliberate attempt to get away from the subject of May Tabor. "If she was around the house so much and the Professor took such a shine to her, it's even odder none of you has ever mentioned her," she said. "In a few well-chosen words from your own book, can you tell me just why this long silence? Or is it something you feel you can't say in front of the children?"

She hadn't expected George to look rattled and while he was saying no, no, it was nothing like that, she began to wonder if perhaps it was very much like that. "It was rather involved," he said, "on account of Laura."

"I guess you're right," said Sally. "There isn't time now. It will be eightish before we know it and I would like to take a bath. Would it be too much to ask you Cutters to tidy up for the company?"

Brad said dibs on washing. When Brad saw there was no way out, he made the best of the situation. He said Mr. Gibson had got a swell new dishwashing machine and had saved a pile of dough by installing it himself. George, sighing his martyrdom, left the dining room with one plate. As Brad said, while he stacked a tray, it was essential to get the Old Man out of the kitchen. "I'll tell him to build a fire," said Brad, "and that will keep him busy and maybe I'll have time to fix it up before Bad News gets here."

"Why don't you wear my blue housecoat?" asked Tess, after Brad had gone to the kitchen.

"I'm not supposed to tell you yet," said Sally, "but Mrs. King says Doctor has his eye on Jack."

"I know, I know," said Tess. "It's all we talk about. But suppose Doc King does take him on? We'll have to wait at least another year. The assistant never gets a fair cut."

"You know Dr. King isn't that way."

"You forget Mrs. King. Now there's a hawk for a dollar. Jack says a year is the absolute minimum. So if you're thinking about the robe, don't bother. I'm not saving anything that long."

"Darling, a year really isn't so very long."

Tess put her cigarette out. Jack didn't approve of smoking women, but a couple of months ago, saying she couldn't keep her weight down any other way, Tess had started to smoke again. "Look who's talking," she said. "How long was it you and Daddy were engaged? Two weeks?"

"Nearly three," said Sally, "but it was different, Tess. He'd already got established in his profession."

"Did you ever stop to think maybe it doesn't make it different all the way down the line?" Tess cleared her throat. She said she guessed she was smoking too much. "Maybe I better switch to marijuana. Go on and take your bath, and wear the robe. I don't like it anyway. Things that rustle give me the willies."

"Then why did you buy it?"

"Dear, the ads always say men go for the sound. Do you think if I'd wear that robe some night . . . ? Of course I'd have to say I had a headache or something, and then we'd be off for a jolly evening of diagnosis." Tess got up and began to collect the place mats. "Sometimes I wonder if things would be different if I had an apartment of my own, but I don't know. . . . It's wonderful how the study of medicine can sublimate sex. I sure made a mistake when I didn't go on with that earthworm in freshman zoology."

Nine

TWO WEEKS AGO when she was doing a thorough job on the closets, Sally would have noticed Tess's blue housecoat if it had been at the back of the closet where it now sagged from a hook. It wasn't like Tess to treat an expensive garment this way. Might she have demoted the robe last Friday after Jack left? Her mother had been in a mood to demote Jack.

On that occasion nothing had gone well. Even more conscious than usual of Jack's disapproval, Sally, carving, had said she was afraid she wasn't a good surgeon. As soon as she said it she remembered she had made this remark at least once before when Jack had dined with them, and she resented his appreciative chuckle, a response of his that was growing more and more professional.

Before Jack's first meal in this house, Tess suggested it might be a good idea to have Daddy carve. "Maybe I'm wrong," she said, "but I think this Russak boy might shy away from a family that looks like it was run by a woman."

"Looks like?" asked Sally. "Looks like what is."

"I know," said Tess, "but I'd rather have him get it gradually. He's not just another date, Mother."

So Sally informed George that he was to preside over the meat. "I'll slice it in the kitchen," she said. "Then, after you've served the meat, you pass the plates down to me and I'll do the vegetables. Surely vegetables are feminine enough."

"Yes, yes," said George. And when they sat down at the table, he commented that the plates were at the wrong end. "Brad," he said, "take these down to your mother. Mr. Russak, will you put this platter down at Mrs. Cutter's end? There seems to be room."

"In just a few months it will be Dr. Russak," said Tess. "Isn't it thrilling?"

The thrill of it probably took Jack's mind from the serving process. Afterward Sally told Tess she was sorry, she'd tried, Daddy had appeared to understand. Actually, aside from the meat business, he hadn't done too badly, had he? He had made very few puns and, luckily, the guest hadn't seemed to get all of those. Brad had done pretty well, too, hadn't he, and his hands had been very clean. Tess, with Jack nailed down for another date, said it hadn't been too awful. And didn't Mother agree that Jack was out of this world? Mother did.

Sally fell hard for Jack Russak. He was handsome, and dark enough to set off Tess's blondness, not an entirely natural state but very becoming. Maybe Jack wasn't tall enough to give Tess the precious look the women's magazine illustrations indicated a requirement for ideal mating, but Jack was in the upper bracket of average-height men. And anyway Tess hated extreme heels.

Jack had a pleasingly deep, soft voice, and old-school manners no woman would be so idiotic as to criticize. He also had the air of quiet authority the magazines said gave a girl a feeling of security. And, my goodness, the way Tess looked at that boy proved how starved she'd been for quiet authority. Her father was quiet at the wrong times and his field of authority was one that bored Tess. Tess was mad about medicine. If her mother had realized what a scientific mind the girl had, she certainly wouldn't have allowed Tess to drop out of college after just the one year.

Along with Tess, Sally was in seventh heaven when it became evident that Jack was as serious about Tess as he was about medicine, or nearly. There was one aspect Sally would have liked to take up with her daughter, but she knew that young people wished to think they had invented sex and that it embarrassed them to have old folks speak familiarly of it. Sally had never been able to tell Tess the facts of life; Tess was the one who did the telling. "You see, Mother," she had said at fourteen, "it's different now."

But just imagine getting sex appeal as obvious as Tony Cado's, *and* brains, *and* an admirable ambition. Of course Sally realized that her own reactions had no bearing on the case, but as time had passed she had begun to wonder if perhaps Tess was also thinking no sex appeal was strong enough to compensate for the ponderous ambition contained in Jack's head. As his bedside manner had been more and more perfected, his ability to have spontaneous reactions appeared to deteriorate. The books Tess provided for her mother's instruction were as specific as Culbertson's rules for bridge, but Sally, clinging to primitive ideas, couldn't help thinking Tess was somewhat like her.

Last Friday George brought the newspaper to the table. He read manuscripts and proofs on the train but sometimes would glance at a newspaper at home. He didn't keep up very well with foreign and domestic policy; he knew nothing about the current murders or the doings in Hollywood; he had disgraced Brad by asking, in Peter Gibson's presence, what team Little Abner played on. But George was a bear on letters, letters to the editor, letters to the beauty and love departments, letters to the child-guidance clinicians; George knew all about "Anxious" and "Worried" and frequently shared his knowledge.

"Listen to this one," he said while Sally hacked at the lamb. "I wish I had started a file of these things. Here's one from 'Fair Play.' If I were a novelist I would write a book and call my heroine Fair Play. Miss Play, daughter of Mr. Play and Mrs. Play. Rather nice?"

"And Fairy to her intimates," said Tess.

"Very good," said George.

"The word has taken on some significance you probably don't know about," said Tess.

"Is that so?" asked George.

"Look, Dad," said Brad, "it isn't something you talk about in mixed company."

Not even Jack could have guessed that this remark had come from the boy who, only a few months ago, had been taken gently aside and informed that his use of the word "fairy" was indiscriminate. "Listen, bub," Tess had said to Brad, "girls aren't fairies." Brad had retorted that out at high school a lot of girls sure were, but last Friday, not being at school, he had been willing to go along with out-of-date connotations.

"I hadn't known there was anything forbidden to mixed company," said George. "Perhaps I should do some cutting. She gives background material on her height and weight which indicates a girl of considerable substance. Quote: 'I don't hardly eat anything but my folks charge me the same board like they did before and I don't think it's fair. They say I'm spoiled but how could I be when they still charge me the same as my brother who does.' End quote."

"Who does what?" asked Sally, to prove she hadn't been married all these years to George for nothing.

"Aren't you going to read the answer?" asked Brad.

But George had dropped the paper to the floor. "I never read the answers," he said. "I like to make them up for myself. Dear Miss Play—it's a family newspaper, Tess . . . Dear Miss Play, You should be charged double. Nothing is more unpleasant for one who does than the presence of one who doesn't. Wouldn't you agree, Doctor?"

"Well, sir," said Jack, "I'm afraid we've pretty well closed the case against obesity." He chuckled when he said this. Oh, Jack was more fun than a pile of monkeys and he was jocular in his presentation of the lean rats' burial of the fat rats, and perhaps even jocular in his mention that his own sisters had never been permitted to pay board.

"Doctor," said George, "how do you stand on votes for women?"

Jack didn't take this in the ugly spirit in which it had been given. "You know, Dr. Cutter," he said—he was wonderful about calling George Dr. Cutter, though Sally knew it must have hurt him every time he said it, "I rather think we went a bit overboard on some aspects. The psychological and physiological differences between men and women would seem to remain unchanged."

"And who decided what those differences were?" asked Tess. "A bunch of fascist fairies."

It was a wonderful housecoat, a hostess gown for special occasions, a robe worthy of inclusion in a trousseau. The taffeta was threaded with hairs of metal that, catching the light, looked like sun-struck water. The fullness was concentrated toward the back and so the robe's length wasn't too bad on Sally. The train looked as if it might have been designed and it was just as well to have the front long enough to conceal black silk slippers that were beginning to be shaggy. Bearing Mrs. Johnson's afternoon costume in mind, Sally decided she didn't look too theatrical. She opened Tess's ribbon box and wondered if the tangle would have made a man of science nervous.

Six months ago Tess had laughed about Jack's refusal to let her carry any of their future financial load. "Boy, I didn't know what an old-fashioned flower I'd plucked in the garden of love," she told her mother. "I went to him all shining with my new gold and said I'd got this marvelous raise, gad, the income tax, but I said maybe I could take him as an exemption for a year or so. How dumb can I get? I thought he meant it wasn't enough and I asked since when he'd got delusions of grandeur, I said this would do it in more style than he'd been accustomed to, people support large families on less. And he said yes, he supposed his family would have to get along on less for a while. He said it might be five years before he'd be earning that much."

"He surely wouldn't expect you to wait that long," said Sally.

"No, he says we can get along on less, a smart girl like I, see. Gad, I mustn't say that. Somehow he's found out it's wrong. Oh, hell, it isn't funny, anyway, and so skip it. He doesn't want me to count on anything, but he says with the breaks, such as Doc King not dropping dead for a while, maybe we can swing it in about a year and a half, provided Doc King does drop dead or out of the picture once he's sewed up."

"I wish you wouldn't talk that way about Dr. King," said Sally. "He's practically a relative. But doesn't Jack know that these days almost every girl works for at least a while after she gets married?"

"He says the prevalence of drunk driving doesn't alter the fact that it's bad business to drive when drunk." Tess said Jack had all the answers, but at that time she still seemed to be getting a kick out of his replies. She said she wasn't taking Jackie-boy quite so seriously as he was taking himself. Six months ago she was confident that she could, if not twist Jack around her finger, at least bend him a little.

But she never would have taken this blue robe out of its protecting bag if she hadn't lost some of her confidence. Her mother's guess was that the engagement wouldn't last much longer.

Sally herself was fed to the teeth with Dr. Russak and never again would she say Tess was lucky to have a man who would discuss his business with her. Tess's enthusiasm for medicine had waned and she no longer blazed out at Brad when he called her Doc. "Kid, you said right," she would say now. Reminded that a while back she had seemed to be asking for it, she said a pre-med course would have satisfied her.

Several days ago, at dinner, Brad asked her to perform an appendectomy on a baked potato. It was an amusing routine she'd gone through for them before, after making them promise not to tell Jack, but this time she shook her head. "Son," she said, "we are now specializing in gynecology and between you and me, it's not for the dinner show. But don't think we don't get it there." She went on to tell them about Arthur and Nancy and Jack. Arthur and Nancy were Jack's friends and fellow interns at the hospital. There was nothing Arthur and Nancy and Jack liked better than getting cozy with shop talk in a restaurant.

"Now and then I have to check my hamburger," said Tess, "to make sure it isn't a tumor they've just finished removing."

Seeing how much George enjoyed this, Sally said she wished he and his colleagues would treat her as if she had enough intelligence to sit in on their shop talk. "All your father's friends ever talk to me about is the weather," she said.

"People should talk more about the weather," said George. "The Professor took a vital interest in weather and . . . "

"A wife is supposed to take an interest in her husband's

business," said Sally. "All the experts say so, but how can I when you won't let me?"

"Now, Mother," said George.

One of these days when he called her "Mother" he was going to get something thrown at him. . . . What's the matter with me? she asked her reflection in Tess's mirror. Aside from looking like a fool with a ribbon around her head . . . What had Dr. King meant about the hat, really? Removing the ribbon, she wished she could so easily remove the internal decorations she found alien and unbecoming. It seemed to her that in striving for the least common denominator, Dr. King had produced a symbol that was as insulting as it was superficial. Did she, then, wish the doctor had prescribed a new husband?

Horrified by the thought, she looked away from the mirror and with less success tried to look away from memories of Tony. After twenty-five years a woman simply could not brood over an ancient love that had been puppy at best and shameful at worst. Not if she was in her right mind.

"Sally," called George from the lower hall, "there's a car pulling up in front."

"You don't say," said Sally, but not loudly enough for him to hear. "I'd thought she would come in a carriage." With purple fringe around the top.

She rolled Tess's ribbon up and returned it to the box. When the porch trembled, she remembered she must do something about that floor. If she put it off much longer and someone as heavy as Mrs. Johnson had a nasty accident, would they prove that Sally had been negligent?

Mrs. Cutter, you admit you knew the porch floor was in bad condition?

Yes, but I was too poor to have it fixed and keep up the insurance at the same time.

Mrs. Cutter, is it true that your father is C. J. Bradford?

Yes, but my husband is a proud man and he won't let me accept financial assistance from . . .

"Well, well," came George's voice, "if it isn't old May!"

There was a whoop and then a smacking sound. Old George had got kissed. Clutching her stomach to suppress hysteria, Sally wondered if he was looking as he always looked on New Year's Eve.

There was a story, not true but gleefully accepted as truth by all who knew George and Patricia, that one New Year's Eve when Patricia asked George if he was going to kiss her, he said she would have to ask Sally.

"Sally!" yelled George now. "We've got company!"

Oh, he was willing to share his memories with his wife now. He was ready to turn them over to her.

Ten

THE BLACK GLOVES ON the hall bench warned that colorwise tonight's Mrs. Johnson might not be stimulating. Away from its purple companions, the mink coat was merely silver-blue, but the mundane habiliments in the hall did not prepare Sally adequately for the discreet dowager in the living room. Tonight's Mrs. Johnson was an unremarkable, which meant exact, copy of how the older Brentwood woman should dress. She was wearing one of those black silk uniforms with the beige lace and net top, dressy enough, the salesgirls always said, but not too-you-know-what-I-mean. Without the jutting frame of feathers, edged only by soft gray hair, Mrs. Johnson's face had lost its orchidaceous high lights and violet shadows; it was just a face with little make-up, no hollows and few wrinkles; it wasn't a bad face. But her eyes are too close together and they're definitely squinty, Sally told herself while she and the guest shook hands. She had to admit, however, that there was no visible excuse, tonight, for George's years of secrecy. Standing beside George Cutter, Mrs. Johnson didn't even look especially large.

"Sally, for heaven sakes, call me May," said the woman. "After all, it isn't as if we were strangers."

The presence of that diamond bird was comforting. Tess would notice the pin and later on she and Sally could say what a bore it must be to have to wear those same old diamonds day and night. Having assured May it certainly wasn't as if they were strangers, Sally asked Brad to do something about the fire. Brad said once Dad had done something, it was quite an assignment.

"George, I always told you it was a pity you hadn't been a Boy Scout," said May in an only-yesterday voice.

"It's the wood Sally's been getting," said George. "It won't burn."

"Tess, dear, would you pass the cigarettes?" asked Sally.

"Such tall children for such a little mother," said May. "Is your other boy a young giant, too? I was so sorry we didn't have a chance to get in touch with him, George, but of course we'll be running back and forth and I suppose he's out here quite often. When Bert comes and we get settled, I want all of you . . . " It looked as if the subject of Nick's height had been safely passed, but after a while May returned to it.

"Couldn't I get some brandy or something?" asked Tess. It hadn't sounded like an interruption, only the sweet young thing's eager attempt to help entertain.

May said a drop of brandy would be delightful. She explained that she had been missing her evening stimulant, that she and Bert, though by no means topers, did enjoy their little cocktail. She said the Abbotts were the dearest people in the world and she adored them, but they were a little . . . "You know. And I never did care much for tomato juice."

Well, well, said George, and he supposed she was still being difficult about Italian food that had tomato, but he interrupted his reminiscences about spaghetti to tell Tess not to bring him anything to drink. He had work to do.

"Oh, Georgie," said May, "you haven't changed a bit."

"Later, I mean," said George.

May could have given Sally credit for having changed him somewhat, at least he had tacked on the "later," but he lacked the manners to refrain from looking at his watch.

"Such a beautiful girl," said May when Tess had left the room. "It's so interesting to see people's children. Tess and Brad resemble both of you, except in height. They're both Cutters when it comes to that. Is your other boy . . . "

"Nick had polio when he was fourteen," said George.

"He takes after my people," said Sally. "We're all middling to short and even if Nick hadn't got sick, he . . . "

"He came down with polio just as he was beginning to get his growth," said George. "If it hadn't been for that, he'd be as tall as Brad."

"Taller," said the loyal Brad.

"I remember hearing he was ill," said May and her face showed great distress, "but I had no idea it left . . . "

"Just a slight limp," said Sally. She didn't know why she always said this. Nick's limp was not slight; he was very lame and would have got around better, his mother thought, had he been willing to continue with the canes or anyway with one cane. But she had to remember that the stubbornness that made Nick quit canes was what got him out of bed, out of a wheelchair and eventually off crutches. Nick's stubbornness and Dr. King. "God damn it, Sally," Dr. King had yelled at her, "take your hands off that boy!"

It had not been Dr. King's case, but he had come around to check on the boy's progress. Nick had been one of his babies and it had always been hard for Dr. King to let go. Hard? As far as Sally could see, he had never tried. Many times during that long siege she had wanted to tell Dr. King to stay away, but what good would it have done? She'd been one of Dr. King's babies, too.

Dr. King and Nick drove the specialists and Sally crazy. Just about when it looked as if Nick was going to co-operate better, old Dr. King would come around to tell the boy that doctors didn't know much about anything. "Spit in their eye, kid," he would say. "You'll be walking when they're dead."

May was saying if she had a son of military age she was afraid she would be grateful if there was some disability. Sally said she felt that way about it, too.

"You don't have to be able to walk a million miles," said Brad. "He could be technical or propaganda or something, with his brains. The creeps don't know what they're doing."

Now Tess came with the tray and also with the cat. What could she do? she asked. When she'd tried to kick him back into the kitchen he had bitten one of her ankles. "And he knocked the cube tray out of my hands, as I imagine you heard."

"He jumps into the refrigerator," Sally explained to the

guest. "Just jumps without looking to see if there's a place to land. I never knew a cat to be so impractical."

Brad said he thought landing on a chicken or something was very practical and May said she adored cats, she would have dozens but Bert was allergic. "Come here, you clever pussy, what's your name?"

"Atom," said Brad.

"He really isn't our cat," said Sally.

"No," said Tess, "he just happened to be passing by four or five years ago."

"Tess, if we were going to have a cat, we wouldn't have such a hideous one," said Sally. "I wouldn't pet him, May. He has a terrible disposition."

"Why, no he doesn't," said May. "Just listen to him purr."

"That's not purring," said Brad. "That's tuning up for the big push."

"Nobody in the market for a cat would ever pick out one with such sinister markings," said Sally. "That black mask across his eyes . . . My grandmother always says all calico cats are female. For five years she's been warning us about kittens."

"I told you what to do," said George. "You know what I said in the beginning."

"I certainly do," said Sally. "I was looking up the Humane Society's number when you said it. Give the poor beast his last supper, you said. Tess, that's plenty if it's for me."

"Sally, those people find homes for them," said George.

"Not for one this ugly," said Sally.

"He had two ears then," said George. "I admit you waited too long."

Brad, coming to collect his Coke, gave a warning cry but the cat had already leapt into the guest's lap and was striking at the diamond pin. "Good gracious," said May after the rescue had been effected, "I wouldn't have thought an artificial bird . . . "

"Oh, it wasn't the shape," said Brad. "You ought to see him go for the Christmas tree. Come on, Atom. A tom, see."

"Thanks for small favors," said Tess, but May said she was glad to have the name explained. She said it was really very clever.

"Yes," said George, "not bad at all."

"I was so terribly sorry to read about your father's death," said May. Brad's pun had, of course, reminded her of Professor Cutter.

"He died in his sleep," said George. "He was nearly eighty and he was active up to the very last. He lectured the day before."

May said it was difficult to realize that the Professor had been that old. "I keep forgetting how long ago it was," she said. "I always kept up with his articles and books. I almost wrote to him several years ago when it seemed to me his name was appearing on the letter heads of some very questionable organizations."

"He had the one rule about joining things," said George. "He would join anything so long as it never held a Chicago meeting."

"But things were different then," said Sally. "I mean, people weren't so intense. These days you almost hesitate to say you belong to the League of Women Voters."

"Do you? I hadn't noticed." Smiling at May, George explained that Sally was a great little League worker. Then he and May both smiled at Sally, the way people smile at an animal that has learned to walk on its hind legs.

"But tell me about the rest of the family," said May.

George looked at his watch. He held it up to his ear. "Been having trouble with this watch," he said. "I have to give it a shake now and then." Apparently he had noticed his daughter's scowl. His wife hadn't frowned at him. No sir, Sally had decided to let old George and old May slug it out for themselves. They were such intellectuals, such soul mates, let them get along without assistance.

Tess lacked her mother's endurance. When it looked as if George would never answer a question, Tess would answer it. Even Brad helped out, but Sally just sat back and smoked.

Surveying the room, she wondered if it struck May as being provincial or primitive. Helen Cutter, artist, hadn't been able to decide which of the two moods dominated the living room after Sally finished the new draperies and slip covers. Patricia had said the room was quaint: "Darling, it's just too quaint for words," she had said. "I don't know how you do it." Patricia had meant Sally to take this as a compliment.

Helen Cutter was not devious or dishonest. Helen wanted people to know exactly what she thought. Not asking Helen for an opinion did not prevent you from getting it. And as so often appeared to be the case with the truth advocates, Helen's thoughts about the creative efforts of other people were unfailingly negative. "Not even good primitive or good provincial," said Helen of the room Sally had slaved over for weeks.

"I've always adored Grandma Moses," said Sally, in defense of the room. "I think it's wonderful you can get it on cloth."

Helen had said she must do something about Sally. She said she never should have let Laura monopolize so much of Sally's education.

May Johnson was talking about the Cutter girls now and saying that although she and Helen were more of an age, she had known Laura better. "Laura and I were really quite chummy there for a while," she said.

Sally and Laura had been quite chummy for a while, too. It was the strangest friendship Sally ever had. She had never exactly hated Laura, she just hadn't liked her very well; but even at the height of the friendship she had felt that Laura rather more than disliked her. And yet Laura was the one who forced the friendship into its brief, unnatural bloom.

The two had gone through high school together. There were two hundred in their graduating class, too many to know each one intimately, but not too many to know by sight. When Sally saw Laura on campus and in a couple of her classes at the University, she assumed they would say hello, but after a few snubs she had stopped trying to speak to Laura. Who cared if Laura Cutter didn't remember or choose to recognize? She was a queer duck, so tall and thin, so regally topped with coronet braids. She was always alone. Sally Bradford was seldom alone, and she was too busy to think about Laura Cutter, but toward spring Laura suddenly called to her on campus. "We're having some people in Sunday night," she said when she caught up with Sally, "and I thought you might like to come."

"Why?" asked Sally. It wasn't the way she had been taught to respond to an invitation, but she hadn't been in a normal state—this was just after the shattering break with Tony.

"Our Sunday nights are considered rather exceptional," said Laura.

Sally knew about the Cutter Sunday nights. It was faculty and graduate-student stuff. She'd never heard of a freshman getting an invitation to one of those highbrow sessions. She knew Laura wasn't so highbrow as she looked. Even in a class of two hundred you eventually found out who were the dumb ones. Laura, Sally knew, just barely got by. She supposed the Cutters permitted their dumb daughter to invite one or two persons so she would have someone to talk to. "We seldom invite undergraduates," said Laura, and Sally, though not wanting to, said she would come. It was at a time when she would have gone anywhere.

Laura didn't make Phi Bete. Sally had heard, and believed, that it was only out of respect for Professor Cutter that Laura had been allowed to graduate from college. Her family always blamed Laura's failure to make good grades on her interest in poetry, but if you asked Sally, who was a most unwilling student of Laura's poetry, the girl might as well have cracked her textbooks.

"Didn't I hear that Laura had a book published?" asked May Johnson.

"She's had several," said George. "How many is it by now, Sally?"

"Eight," said Sally.

Tess murmured that sometimes it seemed like more, but May didn't notice because she was busy gasping her dismay at her ignorance. "Where have I been?" she asked. "Of course I can't say I keep up with the world of poetry. I'm afraid I burned myself out with Millay, but I do try to read the reviews and . . ."

"You're hitting a rather sore spot there," said George. "Sally handles that end. We're always telling her she doesn't promote Laura's things as much as she should. You see, Sally?"

"Should I deliver the copies personally and stand over them with a gun?" asked Sally.

"There's such a thing as promotion," said George.

"Oddly enough that's Aunt Laura's profession," said Tess. "Or perhaps I should say it is the avocation from which she derives her income."

"Laura left the University library about eight years ago," Sally explained to May. "She's with George's company now, in the promotion department."

"You can't expect her to promote her own things," said George. "Anyway, she hasn't the time. You see, May, Sally is Laura's agent."

"How nice to keep it in the family," said May.

"And I've so little else to do," said Sally.

"Matter of fact," said George, "poetry was what brought the girls together in the first place."

"So you write poetry too," said May. "How nice."

"I don't even write a good letter," said Sally. "All I can write is a grocery list."

"Put it in the right type and you've got a poem," said Tess.

May laughed and said she couldn't help feeling a little that way about modern poetry. "I never did understand Laura's poems," she said. "But little did I realize, when she used to read to me, that some day . . . "

"Did you sit on the floor?" asked Sally.

"George," said May, "she's real cute. No, Sally, I didn't sit on the floor. She tried to make me, but I guess I never did have the bohemian spirit."

"The house was too full for everybody to get a seat," said George. "Some Sundays there would be more than a hundred."

"Laura and I used to sit there in the studio all by ourselves," said Sally. "We sat on the floor in front of the fireplace. No fire, though. I remember we always had tea. I suppose it was hot to begin with, but it never was when we got around to drinking it. I've never been so cold in my life."

"Don't pay any attention to her," said George. "She really has good taste. She's done a beautiful job with the books. It's just the promotion that . . . "

"Oh, it hasn't been much," said Sally. "I just go around to all the printers in Chicago and suburbs and get estimates."

She hadn't meant to give away any secret. She wouldn't have thought anyone could believe Laura Cutter did not finance her own publication, but May Johnson's change in expression indicated she had thought so. George, noticing the look, said it was different with poetry. With poetry, he said, one could hardly call it vanity-publication.

May said she knew, she knew. She spoke very sadly of the plight of poets, but she looked pleased. "I was so surprised to hear she didn't marry that What's-his-name," she said. "You know the one I mean, George, the one who was always talking about beetles."

"Beetles?" asked George. "I can't imagine who that could have been."

May said he could, he must, but the subject was postponed. Dr. Russak was at the door.

Eleven

BOTH TESS AND BRAD had dashed for the hall, but Brad wasn't going to the door. He made the mistake of looking over his shoulder just as he was about to skin up the stairs. Sally crooked one finger of the hand she was dangling over the end of the davenport. Brad made an agonized face, but he came back.

He was the only one of her three who had ever been good about obeying a motherly gesture. Recently, at a lecture on "The Obedient Child," Sally had received alarming information that had made her alert for symptoms of schizophrenia in Brad.

You thought you brought them up exactly alike, the speaker had said, but you were mistaken. And he had pointed out so many mistakes that it would have been impossible for each woman in his audience to fail to see herself somewhere in the frightening pictures he presented. Sally, who ached when she read about aches, had seen herself in almost every example. And certainly her three children were very different. Nick wouldn't have had any part of tonight's call. Nick wouldn't have argued, he simply would have gone off. He was so quiet that few people realized how completely self-centered he was. Sally modified the unbidden description: Nick was career-centered. He knew what he wanted and come hell or high water he was going to get it. If you didn't want to get knocked down, you could stand aside. He had always been that way, even before the long illness during which he had, of course, been pampered. It was a Cutter way and deep in Nick's bones even though he looked entirely Bradford.

Tess, between Nick and Brad in character as well as in age, had a mind of her own, but she was willing to listen to another side, to take it under advisement and sometimes to alter her own thinking. Like tonight. She hadn't wanted to stick around, but she had been willing to look at it from her mother's viewpoint and to make the concession. But how many concessions would she be willing to make to the handsome young doctor who made none? For the first time, Sally thought with sympathy of Jack's mother. Did Mrs. Russak blame herself? Or did she think, as Sally thought about Nick, that some things were absolute at birth?

If Nick Cutter and Jack Russak had ever emerged from their specialties during the times they had been together, they might have discovered a basis for friendship. As it was, they acted as if it was necessary for them to speak through an interpreter.

While Jack was being presented to Mrs. Johnson, Brad lit a cigarette. Sally didn't approve of adolescent smoking and it was a subject she and Brad had explored at some length, but now she wished to shout for joy. Brad was showing her there was a limit to how low he would grovel.

"A medical man, Doctor?" asked May Johnson in the special voice some women reserved for the medical profession. It was a tone that lacked the tentative quality of the usual flirtatious manner; a doctor was a sitting pigeon—you could always get sick.

Dr. Russak bowed. Of course there was no reason for him to explain that he was still interning. Perhaps to prevent anybody else from going to this bother, he turned to Brad. "Say, there, young fellow," he said, "aren't you afraid you'll stunt your growth?"

Without thinking, Sally had moved within pinching reach of Brad; it was merely a habit, nothing more than wanting to be in control of a situation. She pinched, not hard enough to make Brad cry out, but hard enough to remind him that she, too, had limits. "No," said Brad, "I figure basketball's on its way out."

"Remind me to give you that cigarette case I never use," said the pleased mother. Maybe the psychologists would have said you shouldn't reward children for refraining from assaulting guests in the home, but Sally felt Brad had earned a present.

"Sit down, Jack," said Tess. "Will you have a Coke?"

Jack said he was sorry, but he was afraid he and Tess would have to rush off. Dr. Hawes was waiting outside. No, thank you, Dr. Hawes wouldn't come in; they were on their way to pick up Dr. Ashland. These were the interns commonly known as Arthur and Nancy, but perhaps Mrs. Johnson's presence did require the more formal approach.

"I didn't know we had a date with them," said Tess. "Gad,

I hope there's not a wreck or something, with all three of you away from the hospital at one time."

Miss Tess should have received her motherly pinch. It was all right for her to object to Jack's increasing habit of never consulting her about their plans, but it wasn't all right for her to do this in front of other people. It wasn't unique for the three interns to be off at the same time; it was a very well staffed hospital. Tess had gone rather far out of the way to make it clear that Jack, though indeed a medical man, was not as yet out on his own. But pinched or not, Tess was headed for big trouble with Jack, and perhaps the sooner it came, the better. Certainly there was no love in the look the engaged pair was exchanging.

May was saying she couldn't get over feeling she'd seen Tess somewhere before. "I don't mean the resemblance to your parents," she said. "Ever since I stepped into this room, it's been bothering me. Is there some actress?"

It was an old story by now. Sally reached for the stack of magazines on the coffee table shelf. The magazine with Tess's lavender picture undoubtedly was the one that had attracted May, the purple lover.

"Why, of course," said May when she took the magazine. "I had this on the train coming out. My heavens, what a remarkable resemblance."

"You sad it, you sad it," said Brad. "The way those creeps operate, it's an iracle-mish."

"A picture that looks like Tess, is Tess," said George. "It's her business." For the first time in his life, as far as Sally knew, George was puffing himself out over the display of his child's photograph.

Tess asked if she might have her father's statement in writing, and May said she was thrilled, she had never met a model before. "And here I thought you were still just a school girl!"

"I thought it was a good idea to quit before I flunked," said Tess.

Brad nodded. "So now it comes out," he said, and blew a disconcertingly perfect smoke ring.

Twelve

AFTER TESS AND JACK had gone, May Johnson looked at the magazine again and said she couldn't understand it. "I would be proud," she said. "I'd be tickled pink."

"She was exaggerating," said George. "She always made her grades. If she had applied herself . . . "

"George, you always forget she has a mother, too," said Sally, "but May isn't talking about that."

"Of course not," said May. "I shouldn't have said anything. Bert's always saying I talk first and think later, but the look on that young man's face startled me so. I suppose modeling does seem frivolous to a doctor, especially to such a young one."

"Especially when he isn't one yet," said Brad.

"Brad, dear, Jack has his M.D.," said Sally, and George commented that he had heard rumors to that effect.

"Are they engaged?" asked May. "He's the best-looking boy I've seen in many a moon, present company excepted."

"Good Lord, May," said George, "you *have* changed. But Tess is a long way from getting serious. She isn't ready to settle down yet."

"To hear him, you'd think she was sixteen," said Sally.

"I resent that," said Brad.

"Resentment noted," said George.

"My, how you two take me back to the old days when it was the Professor and the young George," said May. "Well, looks aren't everything and anyway a girl as beautiful as Tess doesn't have to be in any hurry." Then, without bothering with a pause that would have made the transition less obvious, she said she was still trying to think of the beetle-boy's name. George must know the one she meant, the one Laura had been engaged to.

"You couldn't mean Tommy Gregg," said George.

"That's it," said May. "Tommy Gregg. Why, George, you know they were engaged. Everyone knew it."

"Yes," said George, "but naturally I thought you meant someone else. You couldn't have forgotten Tom."

"Heavens, I haven't," said May. "It was just his name. Why, Sunday night after Sunday night that boy would orate on and on about his precious beetles . . . "

"He was in anthropology," said George. "Still is. He teaches at California."

May said she did not recall that Tommy Gregg had ever talked about anything as interesting as people. "It seems to me I remember wondering if he'd picked zoology because of his looks. George, you know he looked like a beetle. It's all right to say it now, isn't it? I mean, Laura didn't marry him."

"Tommy went to Columbia the semester after you left," said George, "but of course you knew that."

Frowning, May said perhaps she had heard it. "Maybe you did mention it in a letter."

"But you knew it after he got there," said George.

"George, it's a big school," said May. "I don't remember knowing any of the zoology crowd, all right, anthropology. I didn't socialize much and then I dropped out. Along toward spring, I . . ."

But George wasn't waiting for someone else to take over now; George was interrupting. Although he turned the conversation into a channel one would have expected him to enjoy, his summary of Thomas Gregg's *Man Through the Ages* lacked enthusiasm.

"Perhaps he should have stuck to beetles," said May when the lecture was finished.

"You sad it," said Brad.

"May, he could not stick to them," said George. "He was never attached to them."

"Then he should have been," said May. "Was that why Laura didn't marry him? On account of his looking like a beetle?"

Brad's sigh reminded Sally that it was a school night. She said she knew the guest would excuse him.

"Brad's our prodigy," said George. "I used to think it was Tess. She could study while listening to the radio, but Brad has her beat. He can study while watching television."

"Brad, when we're settled I wish you'd come over and see what you think of our set," said May. "Bert says it's the best on the market but I still think it's like looking into a fish bowl, or would it be more like being in the bowl and looking out?"

Waving his long arms, Brad explained the television deal, but finally he excused himself. And then May said George must go about his business, too. "If I know old Midge," she said, "they're going to be late. You know Midge."

"Midge?" asked George.

May laughed. "There!" she said. "We're even. Now you've forgotten one of the old gang. But, George, you couldn't have forgotten Midge Brown. You knew her a lot better than I ever knew Tommy Gregg."

For some reason this made George turn red. With anger? Sally wasn't taking any chances. Although it had been interesting to see how quickly these two old flames could flare up again, the conflagration, she felt, should be kept under control. She explained that after so many years of knowing Midge Brown as Mrs. Abbott, George had got out of the habit of thinking of her as Midge.

"Abbott?" said George. "I don't know any Abbotts."

"In your position I would cherish the name," said Sally. "Mr. Abbott is the one at the bank who was so sweet about fixing things so you wouldn't have to go to prison."

George said he didn't know what his wife was talking about.

"He can add nicely," Sally explained to May, "but he simply cannot subtract."

"Oh, that," said George.

"Yes, that," said Sally. "It was very embarrassing, but Mr. Abbott was wonderful about it."

"That's what they pay him for," said George. "But, May, I don't remember that he was ever around the house."

"His wife," said Sally.

"Midge," said May. "Midge Brown. George, we used to double-date with them all the time, not Al Abbott—it was before Al's time. She was going with Skeet. Now don't tell me you've forgotten Skeet."

"Good old Skeeter," said George. "I wonder what ever became of him."

"So does Midge," said May. "But you go on to your deadline, my boy. Your wife and I have twenty-five years of catching up to do. Midge said nineish. Midge also says she's fortyish and you know we're all in our fifties—oh, not you, Sally. George, you scoot. You've been looking at your watch ever since I came."

"Been having trouble with it," said George.

"Go away," said Sally. "We want to sit here and get quietly drunk. More brandy, May?"

"Well, if you happened to have some bourbon," said May. "Bourbon's really my drink, I mean, if you happen to have any."

So George was dispatched for the makings of a tall drink, and after Sally had followed him to the kitchen, to tell him where she kept the ice cubes, she kicked the cat out onto the back porch and told George to go to his study. Finally she and May settled down in a stillness that must have made the guest a little apprehensive, too. She asked if George's study was upstairs.

"It's off the kitchen hall," said Sally. "I suppose it was meant for a maid's room. Can you imagine anyone being crazy enough to put a maid's room in this house?"

"Doesn't he use a typewriter any more?" asked May.

"Yes," said Sally, "but he's probably doing proofs or something tonight." She didn't say she knew George's door was open, that it was impossible to shut that door quietly, but the guest kept her voice down.

"You wouldn't know how it is to be as tall as I am," said May. "He was the only boy I ever went with that I could really look up to and I don't mean figuratively. That sort of thing didn't interest me much in those days. I was more interested in shoes. With feet as big as mine you just die to wear high heels."

Looking down at May's feet, Sally saw that her heels were very high. That was funny, because somehow Sally had pictured Bert Johnson as being a small man. Hadn't there been a trace of the patronizing tone, in Midge Abbott's voice, that women often used when speaking of short men? But May was saying that she'd never got over George, really.

"Maybe I shouldn't say it to you," she said, "but my stomach acted up when he opened the door."

"I know what you mean," said Sally. "It wasn't height with me, of course, but it was something just as silly. I used to go with the most dreadful character just because he was good-looking. I know if I ever saw him again and he was still that dreamy, my stomach would act up, too. Why do you suppose they always say heart? I guess stomach sounds too unromantic."

"I'm not so sure it's the stomach, either," said May, "but philosophy was my line, not anatomy. Such a waste of time and money, and to think I worked my own way! I don't know why getting stuck on the Professor made me think I could be a philosopher. . . . I'll never forget the last time I saw George.

It was in the fall, when I was leaving for New York. We had lunch at Field's and then we took a cab over to the station."

Sally understood very well why May would remember the cab part. Had George, she wondered, first looked into the streetcar possibilities?

"I remember us standing in the station. It's like a picture you take out of an old album. I even remember what I was wearing—unfortunately." Saying she would freshen up her drink, May added an impressive amount of whisky to her glass. "I love Midge, but my God how tired I am of her operation. She talks and she talks, and gets hurt if I lock the bathroom door. Well, I got over being sensitive about my size. With Bert there just wasn't any use, of course. He's so much shorter, you see. I think if you can't have one enough taller, it's better to have one so much shorter that there's no use to slump or to wear flat heels. If Tess marries that boy, I hope she won't hump over, the way so many women do when they marry short men."

Well, now, Sally wouldn't have called Jack a short man. "I know he looks shorter," she said, "but actually . . ."

"They always look shorter," said May. "That's why I never got entirely over George. I hope you don't mind."

"I'd feel awful if you hated him."

"God knows I tried to. And you, too. Well, that part of it didn't take much trying and of course Midge was helpful. She kept writing about how you were Freshman Beauty Queen."

"Politics," said Sally. "It was my sorority's turn to win. Our logical candidate wasn't very popular, I guess because of being so absolutely beautiful, and the girls knew we could win with anyone. I've always been ashamed of it, I mean, because the logical girl was my best friend and, golly, I shouldn't have accepted the nomination."

"Being so ugly," said May. "And Midge wrote about how rich you were and popular—everything I'd never been. No, it wasn't hard to hate you. She sent all the clippings from the society columns. I can still tell you what you wore for the wedding."

"Don't," said Sally. "It was ghastly."

"Your grandmother's lace collar and . . ."

"My grandmother is a tyrant. Oh, it was the most gruesome wedding. Everybody was mad at everybody. The Cutters would hardly speak to my family. Laura wouldn't even come."

"Such a strange girl. I often wondered if she . . . But I met Bert that summer and then everything was all right, really all right. It's a crazy thing. He's younger and shorter and we don't agree on anything you'd think people would have to agree on. We go to different churches, cancel each other's votes and we don't even like many of the same foods. I keep thinking it can't last, but . . ."

While May continued to talk about herself and Bert, Sally noticed that however much the woman might say she feared that her marriage wouldn't last, she wasn't looking worried. When had you talked with a long married woman so obviously in love with her husband? Looking away from May, Sally wondered if she resented May's ability to love someone other than George Cutter. Or did May's happiness somehow belittle Sally's marriage? Or did Sally simply resent May's evident ability to retain much of the emotional reaction people usually lost after many years of marriage? There was something about May, when she spoke of Bert, that reminded Sally of how Tess used to speak of Jack.

But, looking at the very pale liquid in her own glass, Sally reminded herself that she had not added to her first very light drink, nor had she finished her brandy. May Johnson, she decided, was slightly drunk.

Weary of the maudlin, Sally remarked that she had never heard of Tommy Gregg until tonight, but when she noticed how quickly May latched on to this information, she altered her idea about how well the guest could carry liquor. "Now that's very interesting," said May. "When I was around, Tom Gregg was certainly like one of the family. If they've never said anything about him, it must have been pretty terrific."

And did this mean that whatever it was in connection with May Tabor must have been pretty terrific? Yes, Sally would have done well to keep that nugget for herself, but of course she would never have to let old May know that she, also, had been news to Sally.

With a gesture of regretful finality May put her glass down. No thanks, she said, she had had just the right amount to see her through another evening with Midge. She looked at her watch and apparently was able to see more than diamonds. The Abbotts, she said, would be coming any minute now and she must be getting into her coat, because like all chronically tardy persons, Midge could not endure to be kept waiting.

Thirteen

THE FRONT AND STUDY doors closed simultaneously. When Sally jerked the study door open, she was kind enough to refrain from going to the desk to see what George had accomplished in his minute of furious application.

He whipped the sheet of paper from the typewriter. Sally smiled when he put that paper face down on the stack of manuscript at his side, but she said nothing. She went to the chair she'd put into this room several years ago in the hope of making the study look less like the storage closet of a badly run book shop. She took the stack of books from the chair and put them on the floor. She lined them up neatly and in answer to George's cry, said she hadn't hurt anything. "They were going to fall off," she said. "No wonder you seldom take books out of a library. I bet you're blacklisted."

"Has she gone?" asked George.

"You know she has. You've been listening."

He gave an abrupt bark that may have been supposed to represent laughter. "If I had been interested in hearing what you said, I certainly would have been thwarted. What were you whispering about at such a great rate? I don't see how you two could possibly have anything in common."

"How modest of you." She brushed the chair off before she sat down.

"Where'd you get the fancy bathrobe?" he asked.

"It is not a bathrobe. It's a hostess gown."

George said it looked like a bathrobe. "See here, Sally, I've got work to do and if we're going to the Smiths' damn party Saturday night . . . "

"Why didn't you marry May?"

George sighed. "God knows I don't want to go to the party. Shall we go into the other room and make ourselves comfortable?"

"Why, George?"

"If you're determined to spend the rest of the evening mulling over the olden days . . . "

"A simple answer shouldn't take all night. Why didn't you marry her?"

"Now who's being modest?" asked George, as if he had read the line in a newspaper letter.

"Laura rammed me down your throat. That's nothing new to me. Of course I see now that Laura was trying to break you and May up. The motive's new to me. I knew Laura didn't want me to marry you. I was just supposed to divert your attention, wasn't I, and then like a good little girl I was supposed to go off about my own business. Evidently Laura wanted to keep the dear little family intact."

George rubbed his forehead. "Do you think so? But she couldn't have done a thing like that."

"A person who writes that kind of poetry is capable of anything, anything terrible. May thinks so, too. She practically said so."

"She did?"

"Not in so many words."

"Well, you couldn't expect her to tell you the whole story, could you?"

"She seemed willing to tell a good deal. Oh, not all of it. I suppose she thinks I'm dumb, but I'm not that dumb."

"Then you think she was lying about Tom? For a minute there, I was inclined to believe she really couldn't remember his name."

"She couldn't, but what's that got to do with it?"

George pushed the typewriter a few inches forward on the desk. "But that would mean the whole thing was an invention. She couldn't have invented a story like that."

Sally said she was unable to see that the story was one which would tax the creative powers. "Zoology isn't such a far cry from anthropology as all that. And he probably did look like a beetle. It's an old cliché, beetle-browed."

But George said he had meant Laura. He asked if Sally thought there was something wrong with Laura. Sally said it was strange it had taken him so long to notice that both of his sisters were rather different from most people, but he said he wasn't talking about eccentricity. He was talking about psychosis. "Laura's always done a competent job at the office," he said. "Nothing brilliant, but I would say adequate. I've told Ann not to hesitate to say so, if she thinks Laura isn't up to the job. After all, it isn't as if I owned the company and had a right to carry a relative on the payroll. Time and again I've asked Ann . . ."

While he continued to talk about the office, Sally found herself thinking she might have known Ann Price would get into tonight's conversation some way. For more than fifteen years it had been Ann-this and Ann-that. It seemed to his wife that George Cutter referred to Ann Price the way many persons referred to the Encyclopaedia Britannica and that whenever the talk became serious, George must always ring in his assistant, his good right hand. Sally agreed it was a blessing he had got so gifted a helper, a person who not only knew what he was thinking but a person who could anticipate what he was going to think. And Miss Price kept track of everything. She made the reservations, bought the tickets, packed the brief cases. . . .

Sometimes when Sally unpacked George's suitcase, she was sure that Ann packed more than brief cases. George couldn't fold things properly and yet very often his suitcases would be as orderly when he came home from a trip as they had been when Sally had sent them out. She had toyed with the idea of saying, very gaily, that taking care of his personal baggage was certainly the ultimate in services provided by his super-secretary who was now assistant editor. But she hadn't dared risk getting an answer. Suppose George said that he had packed his suitcases himself? Or suppose he said what she thought was more likely to come from him, that inasmuch as he was unable to do an efficient job of packing, it was good of Ann to take on this additional chore?

Attending conventions and conferences, going off for meetings with educators, was an important part of George's job. His honeymoon had been spent at a convention. That was why he and Sally had married in such a hurry. George had to go to San Francisco on business, expenses paid, of course; it had seemed a wonderful opportunity to get a honeymoon at half price. They had planned to go to the Grand Canyon before returning home, but an extra session of the conference and the need to get back to the office had prevented them from taking the side trip. When Sally talked about still having that part of the honeymoon coming, George always said yes, they would have to do something about that one of these days.

The San Francisco assignment had been George's first big responsibility. He had had very little public-speaking experience and hadn't wanted Sally to attend the meetings at which he had to talk; he hadn't let her go to any of the other meetings, either. He said she wouldn't be interested, he would be nervous if she was in the room and, anyway, wives didn't go.

Sally spent most of the time in Chinatown and now when people talked about San Francisco's Chinese district, she wondered if she had hit it on an off-season. As far as she had been able to see, all it had over Chicago's Chinatown was size. Of course when she'd had a great deal of time to spend, the matter of size hadn't been negligible. She had thought of looking up a sorority sister who was then living in San Francisco but somehow it hadn't seemed quite the thing to do on a honeymoon and the girl might have thought it odd.

As the company's business prospered, George's need to travel increased, but Sally had accompanied him only on that first trip. Of course she couldn't go along when Nick and Tess were babies, but there had been a period, between Tess and Brad, when she could have got away for a few days at a time. Her mother would have been delighted to keep the children, but George had always said the trips would be unbearably dull for his wife. When she suggested that she might help him, he laughed. For a while he had a male assistant who traveled with him, but the young man simply had not worked out and when Ann Price was promoted to assistant editor, Sally had agreed it was only fair to give a woman an equal opportunity. When she had said this, she hadn't known that the opportunity was to include making trips with the editor. The first time she discovered that Miss Price had gone along on a field trip, Sally asked who else had been in the party. George had said it was bad enough to have him and Ann out of the office at the same time, but that luckily Ann's many talents made it unnecessary for them to take a secretary. The mention of a chaperone certainly would not have fitted in with George's remarks about the travels.

Nevertheless, when her husband continued to stress Ann's importance in the office, Sally seized upon what she considered an opportunity. She said she could learn to do everything Ann did in connection with the trips and then Ann could remain in Chicago where, as George was always saying, she was so badly needed. But George said there was a good deal more to it than Sally realized, that it wasn't simply a matter of making out schedules and buying tickets. Ann knew the business from A to Z, he said. Ann could take over a meeting when there was a conflict, she knew how to deal with writers, she knew all about contracts and the needs of the company. He said he appreciated Sally's offer to learn typing and shorthand but that Ann's job on trips required a great deal more than stenographic competence.

Sally knew her job was at home and that it was foolish of her to think she could catch up with Ann Price just by taking a few trips with George. She hadn't let herself worry about Ann, the way a wife might worry about a girl with whom her husband spent so much time. There was one very comforting thing about this paragon; she was extremely unattractive. When Sally thought about George and Ann being away together, she remembered every detail of Ann's face and figure and she laughed at herself. Ann looked rather like a sheep and for a thin, almost scrawny woman, she had incredibly wide hips. And she didn't do a thing about her hair. From the look of it, she didn't even use a comb. And she wore glasses. Very thick-lensed glasses. The poor girl was probably cross-eyed without her glasses.

"I never told Ann about that business at the library," George was saying now. "I've often wondered if I had a right to keep it from her. Still, I couldn't help feeling Laura deserved the benefit of the doubt, not that Ann would have let a thing like that prejudice her."

"What business at the library?" asked Sally. "You mean the University library?"

"It's the only one Laura ever worked at, isn't it?"

"I never heard anything about a business at the library."

"Of course we had to keep it from the Professor."

"You did a nice job of keeping it from me, too. Didn't Laura resign from the library?"

"Oh, yes, she resigned. I had a talk with Davidson and we fixed that part of it up. He didn't agree with me, but he was willing to go along to a certain extent, on account of the Professor. Well, and knowing he wouldn't be asked to write a recommendation, not when I was to be the next employer."

"But what had she done?"

George shrugged. "The other woman was after her job. Even Davidson saw that. There was no proof one way or another, though, and Davidson chose to believe the other woman. So Laura was out and there was nothing I could do, really. I couldn't even be sure that I was right and yet when everything went so well at the office, I began to think . . . "

"But you didn't tell Ann anything about it?" This seemed to Sally to be far more important than anything Laura Cutter might have done.

He shook his head. "But I can't help wondering, Sally. While May was here, I got to thinking about four promotion people we've let go since Laura's been with us. People fired on her say-so."

"You mean you fired them without asking Ann?"

"The first three were people neither of us had any direct contact with, and I doubt if Ann gave it much thought. She would have said something. Ann doesn't hold anything back from me. But this last case—well, she said she felt we didn't have enough to go on and I agreed with her. I told Laura I felt she was being unfair to the girl in question. She took it all right, or seemed to. She said I was the boss. But then that girl began to turn in such sloppy copy that Ann said there was no alternative, we'd have to get rid of her. It's terrible, Sally, but all evening I've been remembering that girl's copy went through Laura's hands before it ever reached Ann or me."

Heaven knew that Sally didn't admire Laura, but what George was suggesting was too much and she said so.

"I know," said George, "but if she lied about Tommy and May . . . Of course you must remember that May's no fool."

"I'm remembering. Sometimes I can remember things for even more than a day."

"Yes, it would have been clever of May to bring him in that way, as if she couldn't think of his name, as if she'd hardly known him. Not so much on my account, I imagine, but just to make sure I'd never let anything slip around that Bert. Yes, that might be the answer. The other interpretation would mean that Laura is considerably more than eccentric. I think you're wrong, Sally. Laura may be slightly nuts, but she isn't insane."

"Was that my proposition?"

George pulled the typewriter back into position. "Yes, that must be it," he said. "You mustn't underestimate old May. Now run along, dear."

He had typed several lines before Sally told him she was not underestimating old May. "But she's underestimating me a little and so are you. This afternoon I was almost sure you and she had been lovers, but tonight, of course, I knew."

"Well, now, how did you arrive at that conclusion?" George seemed very interested, too interested in what she had said, Sally imagined, to see that she herself wasn't especially interested in it. It was too long ago. For Sally its only immediacy was its relation to Ann Price, the woman whom she was afraid to discuss.

"Well," she said, "I think being lovers gives people a feeling of possession they never quite lose. No matter how hard they try, it's there and they can't entirely hide it. It's different from having been just engaged, without sleeping privileges. There's something about the way you and she look at each other, about the way you talk . . . I can't put it into words. It's a sort of recognition of property, I mean, it's something that's there even though neither of you is interested in remembering or repeating."

Grinning, George leaned back in his chair. "And what chance would I have against such conviction? If I said yes, you would give me hell; if I said no, you'd call me a liar."

"Weren't you and May lovers?"

"You know, my dear, I don't consider that any of your business." He was still smiling.

All right. Sally was willing to have him rule her out of Old Business, but what about New Business? What would he say if she asked about him and Ann? But she didn't dare, she had to keep on with the pretense of caring about May. "Then you were," she said.

He appeared to be delighted. "You see? Exactly what I said. You had it all worked out before you asked. Tell me, dear, how do you know so much about the way lovers look at each other? From observation or from actual experience?"

"Maybe I don't consider that any of your business," said Sally as she got up. "You're a fine one to hop on Jack about the double standard."

"Good for you," said George. "I certainly walked into that one, didn't I? You polish Jack off like that and I'll be content. Damned prig. What does she see in him that she couldn't see at a movie?"

"George, suppose there was some gossip about May and that Tommy." Carefully Sally restored the books to the chair. "I bet it wasn't true. May's not that subtle. She really couldn't think of his name and I'm sure she was telling the truth when she said she didn't see him at Columbia. But that isn't the point. It makes me sick that you didn't give her the benefit of the doubt. After all, she's hardly the kind of person you sleep with and then just forget. I mean, even if she did sleep with you."

"That's a pretty compliment, my dear, though I'm not quite sure for whom."

"You know she wouldn't have, if she hadn't thought you were going to marry her."

"Sally, you fascinate me, but I do have to get this work done."

"Believe me, if I had known what I was breaking up . . ."

"Sally, for once and all, get it through your head. You didn't break up anything. It was finished before I ever saw you. Now, if you expect me to go to that dinner party, for God's sake get out."

George was capable of refusing to go to a party after his wife had said the Cutters would be delighted to come. More than once Sally had had to call up a hostess at the last minute and give some excuse, somebody running a high temperature, that sort of thing. Many persons undoubtedly had caught on.

The Cutters were entirely too healthy looking for people to believe the extreme-illness story very often. And some women had stopped inviting the Cutters. It was a wonder that any invitations, especially for dinner, came this way at all.

"All right," said Sally when she reached the study door, "but in your place I would be very much ashamed of myself."

He looked at her over the top of his glasses. "Okay, Sal," he said. "You win. Call her up in the morning and tell her I'm sorry. I'll marry her just as soon as the divorces are out of the way."

Fourteen

HOLY CATS," SAID Helen Cutter when she opened the door. "Already?"

Helen, social chairman for this house since the Professor's death, had her own special talents for the office. People were always telling Sally how refreshingly bluff and hearty the elder of George's sisters was; it was another way of saying Helen Cutter was loud-mouthed and rude. And perhaps it was also another way of saying she might be a genius whom even Brentwood granted prerogatives. In a world of liars, where the Cutters were so rare, how could one tell what was meant?

"Darling," said Tess, "you make us feel so wanted."

"If you'd just walk in," said Helen, "without standing on the bell."

"Helen," said George, "the door was locked."

"Goodie," said Tess, "now we're going to talk about the lock. Who was it?"

"Some idiot we had in to clean," said Helen. "It had never been locked before but she had to go and monkey around."

George said he believed it was simply a matter of pushing

something. Helen said nothing would push. Tess clucked her tongue. Sally couldn't blame her daughter much. The story of the jammed lock was tiresome, but Tess was old enough to behave herself and to let her father have the next line in this historic dialogue, the suggestion of a drop of oil.

Ignoring Tess's heavy sarcasm, George and Helen said yes, perhaps a drop of oil would do the trick. They looked at Sally, the one who might have an oil can in her pocket. Then, remembering the family now had an even more gifted fixer, they searched the hall for Brad. Sally reminded George and told Helen that Brad was at the Y. "He'll be here pretty soon," she said, "but don't you remember he said you need a new lock?"

"Of course you could take it out," said George. "There seem to be screws."

"But the thing is," said Helen, "would the door stay shut? You wouldn't want it hanging open in winter, what with the price of coal. Have you had your breakfast?"

"We are fifteen minutes late," said George. "We were invited for one-thirty. That wretched man prayed for six minutes, but did he make the time up in the sermon? He did not. He preached thirty-seven minutes and to top it off, made us sing every damn verse of the longest, most erotic poem Adam Levering ever wrote. Let me rest my weary head on Thy Breast, capital T, capital B. I'd give a pretty to see the original manuscript. The Church, my eye. It was some woman." George flung his coat on the window seat.

"If you believe Granny," said Tess, "it couldn't have been Mrs. Levering."

"Poetry of that sort is never written to wives," said George.

"Hot ziggety," said Helen. "Maybe I'm missing something by not going to church. Tell me more."

George said she looked terrible and that she should go clean herself up. Looking down at her paint-splashed apron, Helen asked if religion always put her brother into such a sweet mood. The red that dominated the denim butcher apron was repeated in a streak across her face, and a red-laden brush rested on her right ear. "I was going, really going," she said. "I had no idea what time it was getting to be. I have a show coming up, you may remember."

"I have a few things coming up myself," said George.

"It's different for you," said his sister. "Mine's emotional as well as cerebral." She explained what she had explained many times before: she was no amateur, with the amateur alibi for indolence, that crap about working only when inspired; on the other hand she was no commercial hack who wouldn't know an inspiration if it came with a label. All right, so she was commercial to a certain extent, a girl had to live. She taught; she received money from the Brentwood School of Art; she sold her paintings, or was willing to sell them and she would, you wait and see, if she lived long enough for the rest of the world to catch up with her. Or her heirs would get rich if they played it smart and didn't let collectors do them out of the lot.

Tess tried to speak up here, but Helen wasn't ready to give way. Helen was the first to admit there'd been a time when Helen Cutter was crass as hell. In her artistic adolescence she'd illustrated children's books, God forgive her, and she would thank Tess not to twit her. "You're in no position, young lady."

"You've got red all over your face," said George.

Helen examined her face in the hall mirror. She didn't care about her face, but the blob of paint that had got into her hair worried her. She cherished her wonderful red hair, her creation, her hobby that one day, she said, would make them all rich. The formula for what she called a rinse to bring out her natural red lights, lights nobody else had ever noticed, was Helen's million-dollar secret. When she got around to putting the rinse on the market, she said they would all go to Bali and lie naked in the sand. Helen was always talking about going off somewhere to lie naked.

"Crimson lake?" asked Tess. She and Sally had decided the hair dye was based on crimson lake oil paint.

"Kid," said Helen, "you're getting an eye. One of these days I'll give you a dip. We'll develop the full color slowly, so people will forget you weren't always a redhead. They'll say you got it from your aunt." Proudly she tossed the mane she had raised after deciding a crewcut didn't give the formula enough scope. What Helen had now was a pageboy length and a Dutch-boy style. She hadn't the Cutter curls. Somewhere in the earlier history a Cutter as daring as George must have broken the regal tradition of marrying Cutter.

Under the work apron was a faded blue and white kimono, the sleeves torn away and used, no doubt, for paint rags. The kimono was too short for Helen; everything was always too short for the six-foot woman who had no time for letting out hems and maybe nothing but admiration for her thin legs. It would have been a mistake to assume that Helen had even a fraction of her sister Laura's indifference to personal appearance. Helen was as vain as any normal woman. The difference between her and the ordinary woman was only that the results Helen achieved were extraordinary. Today her toenails were painted turquoise, to match the ribbons that secured her sandals. Sally guessed that what Helen had now gone aloft to get into would be the silver and turquoise complemented representation of the Southwest. Helen dressed as she painted, emotionally and cerebrally; her costumes had titles.

"Cactus Sun," said Sally to Tess.

Tess said this wasn't fair, that she'd been going to guess that outfit. "But never mind, I'll take *Rodeo Day*. There's just a chance that she didn't paint the nails this morning. I just love the sort of ochre she uses for *Rodeo Day*, don't you? It has such an embalmed look."

George had gone on into the studio to see his mother. Brushing dog hairs from his coat, Sally removed it from the window seat to the closet. Which, she asked her daughter, did Tess prefer, dog hairs or mildew? Tess was going on to a party from here. She said she could fit her story to suit the place her mother chose for the coats. "I can say I've been cleaning dog runs, or I can say it's a new perfume my fiancé gave me, a repellent, not that he seems to need it. I wonder if I'm losing the old s.a. The boys at work seem to respond nicely, but it may be professional habit."

"Mothers are supposed to know the right things to say," said Sally as she hung her coat up, "but I don't. I hope you know what you're doing, Tess."

"All I know is that it would have been different if we'd got married a year ago."

Sally shook her head. "He would be the same. He'd still be

interested in the same things and he'd still like Arthur and Nancy. You mustn't expect him to change."

"I'm the one. I'm the one changing. And don't tell me I'm young."

"I won't. I'm sick of hearing you say I was married and had a baby when I was your age."

"Two babies," said Tess. "You're two up on me by now."

"I wonder if a doctor could help you."

"For God's sake, Mother, don't say doctor to me. It's getting so I think of it as being a dirty word."

"I meant a psychiatrist."

Tess laughed. "I wonder how long it would take a psychiatrist to find out what's eating me and how much it would cost. It isn't very complicated. It's just how long can I wait."

"I imagine it's the sort of thing psychiatrists work on right along," said Sally. "I doubt if it would do any good if you went alone. Jack would have to go, too."

"And carry all those coals to Newcastle? He's practically a psychiatrist himself, hadn't you heard?"

"If he knows anything about psychology . . ."

"But he does, he does. He tells me all the time. I just don't sublimate. Do you think I should take up painting or poetry?" Tess put an arm around her mother. "Come on, darling. Don't look so down. I shouldn't blow off to you. Just remember there's always the satisfaction of knowing I won't have to be a virginal old maid. I've got a very good list of prospects and that's always so comforting, don't you think? Poor old things, I don't suppose the aunts wanted it to turn out this way."

"As long as I've known them they've appeared to be very well satisfied."

"Beautiful sublimation," said Tess. "But why did Rita take up sculpture?"

Sternly Sally told her daughter to pull herself together. "Just because you and I lack talent," she said, "it doesn't mean we have any right to say they aren't artistic. Why, people like you and me don't even know what they like."

As they stepped into the studio, Tess asked her mother kindly to speak only for herself.

Fifteen

SO, SPEAKING ONLY for herself, Sally said the small figure on Rita's work table was lovely. It was an adjective that would have sent the former Rita into a tirade but, since her stroke, George's mother had become not only tolerant but actually lovable. Sally thought it a blessing the stroke had come early enough to give the Professor three years of peace, but the old man hadn't seemed to appreciate his good fortune. Many times, after his wife's stroke, he had sighed to Sally that Rita had lost her starch.

The stroke had left little physical disability, but as standing and walking now tired the sculptor, Rita no longer worked on large pieces. Much of her time was spent in Nick's old wheelchair. Brad had constructed a shelf that clamped to the chair and on this cluttered table was today's creation, an object with four legs. George said it didn't look like a unicorn to him. Tess said whatever it was, it was pregnant.

"That's a marvelous idea," said Rita. "Thank you, Tess. It would mean I believe they still exist. Charming. I might call it *Fertility*, oh, ever so many good titles. Sometimes I wonder if I should have written, but it always struck me as being such a confining art; even if you do make up words, like Laura, you are still confined to the alphabet."

"Plus all the possible variations of punctuation," said George. "You know, it looks like Jump."

The mass of gray matted hair that lay in a chair near Helen's easel moved. Near the fireplace, in another large chair, was another mass of gray. The one near the fireplace remained inert and so Sally supposed that one was Hop. She had never been able to tell these identical twins apart.

"Jump, old boy," said George, "she's done a portrait of you."

Rita fussed with the red ribbon that helped to soften the difference between the white of her own hair and the rich brown of her false bangs. "George, you're just like your father," she said. "You have his same keen power of observation. Helen was doing Jump all morning and talking to him so he'd hold the pose. My subconscious must have taken over." The small roll that was to have been a horn was pressed back into the clay can. "So it is finished. I wish I could put it in Helen's show. I always think a show is more interesting if it has more than the one medium."

"Never mind," said George, "we'll have a show just for you."

"I'll wear my Spanish comb," said Rita. "I wonder if I should dye my hair, but I rather like the contrast."

"It's different," said Tess.

"No, don't you remember that conductor at Ravinia?" asked Rita. "The one with the white mustache and the dark hair, or maybe the other way around. So interesting."

George, who had gone to the easel, was squinting at the canvas and saying he saw no dog. "She's stuck a piece of rope down here at one corner," he said. "Oh, I know! Jump, the Rope."

"That's very clever of you, George," said Rita. "So like the Professor. My, how I miss intelligent conversation. Of course the girls are intelligent, but their talk doesn't have much zip, somehow. We'll make a guessing game of it when they come down, about the painting. Helen hasn't much humor when it comes to her work, but by now she should be used to having people guess about her pictures."

"I've a guessing game for you," said Sally when she had removed Rita's table and pushed the wheelchair down toward the fireplace end, the sitting part of the room. There was no fire but on and around the hearth was an accumulation of crumpled paper which George, the fire builder, said would be ample for starting a fire, once they'd got some wood. He and his mother looked tentatively at Sally, but Sally said they would have to wait until Brad came.

"I'm always so impressed by people who have an instinct for what piece of wood is going to burn," said Rita. "My dear, you wouldn't happen to have a cigarette? I finished the very last one in this house just before you walked in."

The Cutter women were heavy smokers. Without their cigarettes, they died. During the war, to keep Helen, Laura and Rita alive, Sally had given up smoking, and somehow the three hadn't got quite out of the habit of looking to their little Sally for the major portion of their cigarettes. Or so it seemed to one who could be very small about small things.

"I'm almost beginning to like your brand, dear," said Rita, after she had got herself comfortable. "Now, give me the first clue for your guessing game and, for once, dear, don't give the answer away before I've had a chance. You never seem to get the idea."

"It's someone who used to come here a long time ago," said Sally. What, she wondered, would May Tabor Johnson think of this room now? Most of the furniture was massive, square-cornered oak, upholstered in brown leather that was flaking and peeling and in some places undoubtedly rotting; but the room had been altered by more than the passage of time. A dozen years ago Helen had toured Mexico and brought back mementoes as well as drawings and paintings. The orientals that used to cover the ballroom floor, laid thirty-five years ago when Laura, incredibly, had thought to replace Pavlova, had been given away, thrown away, maybe just shoved away into a corner of the basement or attic. Now the floor was rumpled with serapes. At the windows hung lengths of Mexican cloth, pinned up for the effect. Helen had been so delighted with the effect that she hadn't wanted to risk taking the cloth down for sewing. She said she'd do the job when the time came for the draperies to be cleaned.

On the concert grand, untuned since the Professor's death, was a slit, stained cape, souvenir of a famous bullfighter's fatal goring, said Helen. Helen had a capacity for believing anything she wanted to believe. Everything she possessed was authentic. Stellar among her possessions was her talent, her genius, and, for all Sally knew, Helen might be a genius. Exposure to the artist robbed one of complacency. As Sally had said to Tess, she no longer knew what she liked. Although she spoke up valiantly in behalf of Grandma Moses, she wasn't sure she really liked her new draperies and slip covers. And, what was more disconcerting, she was no longer sure that she disliked all of Helen's work.

But Rita was demanding further clues. "How long ago?" she asked. "Had the boys been born?"

Staring at Hop, Sally thought back over the sheep dogs. "It was in Potty's day," she said.

"That is going back," said Rita. "Potty was the first. Before that, they were very miscellaneous. Oh dear, Potty tried to continue in that direction. Her first litter, my dear, they weren't human! We never told the children."

"What's that?" asked George.

"Oh, I never meant you to know," said his mother. "But Potty would wander. Some people say it can affect the next litter, too, but I don't believe that. Look at how perfect the boys are. Did Potty like this person?"

"George will have to answer that one," said Sally. "The person likes cats."

"Then it can't be anyone we knew well," said Rita.

"Has the dog book turned up yet?" asked George.

"No, dear, but you know we didn't put people in the dog book and so that wouldn't help," said Rita. "Unless it was a vet? We did put vets in. But we wouldn't have had a vet who was interested in cats. A friend of yours, Sally?"

"I think so," said Sally, "but I met her for the first time last Monday at the parsonage."

"There you go," said Rita. "You tell too much. You've told me it's female and religious. So now I know more than ever that it couldn't be anyone we knew well. Our friends never frequented parsonages. Darling, I know you have to, on account of your uncle. It's such a pity, because otherwise he's a nice little man. Dear me, this really is rather difficult."

"She hasn't given you a decent clue yet," said Tess. "Rita, when this woman called on us Monday night, she kissed Daddy. I didn't see it but I heard it. A real smackeroo."

Although it was tempting to look at George, Sally's attention was held by the expression on her mother-in-law's face. That Rita had guessed was obvious, but was Rita scolding Tess for having given the game away? "Child, that's no clue," she said. "What woman wouldn't kiss your father? Oh, he and the Professor were always great ones for the ladies. My goodness, if I were to guess every woman who'd be likely to kiss your father . . ."

"As a rule you say so, when you've guessed," said Sally.

"But at a parsonage," said Rita. "It's the last place in the world I'd expect her to be. But, Sally, I don't know why you think we didn't like May. We were all very fond of her, weren't we, George?"

George looked up from the magazine he had taken from the floor's collection of reading material. "Did you say something, Rita?"

"He's been very jittery since he got kissed," said Tess.

"Don't be silly," said Rita. "Your father is a man of the world. What I was saying, George, is that Sally gave me an unfair clue. May and Potty were very good friends and you know how Potty was about cat people, wouldn't have a thing to do with them. Well, I always said we hadn't seen the last of May."

"Did you?" asked Sally. "I can't remember ever hearing any of you mention her."

"Nonsense," said Rita. "She was practically one of the family for some years. Has she changed much?"

"I never saw her until Monday," said Sally. "She's come here to live. Her husband's been transferred to Chicago. Her name's Johnson now."

"George, why didn't you ever tell me she'd got married?" asked Rita. "I wonder if it's too late to send her a little wedding gift."

George brought the magazine over to the enormous coffee table that was covered with magazines, dirty ash trays, used paper tissues and little statues. "I couldn't tell you what I didn't know."

"So unromantic of her," said Rita. "Dear, don't put anything more on the table. Put it back where you got it. No, maybe you better keep on looking at it. You give things away and I hear someone coming. Your face gave it away to me. You had your May Tabor look . . . But, not a word." Raising her voice Rita spoke of Jump's morning pose. "But here's Helen and she can answer your question. Helen, dear, George thinks it can't be a portrait of Jump. He thinks perhaps it has something to do with jumping rope."

"I've another idea," said George. "You could call it *Enough*."

"Very funny, I'm sure," said Helen. "It isn't a portrait in the conventional sense, of course, but it will be perfectly clear in sequence. I think I've explained that the show's a psychoanalytical survey. Sally, you should have got those invitations in the mail a whole lot sooner than you did."

"I couldn't send them before they came from the printer," said Sally. "If that secretary at your school hadn't been so slow . . ."

"I told you you'd have to light a fire under her," said Helen. "And you really should have cracked down on that printer. Sal, the trouble with you is you let people walk all over you."

Sixteen

SMOG WAS GRADUally obscuring *Cactus Sun* but the yellow of Helen's tentlike garment, bound at the middle by a thick red wool scarf, was still vibrant. The scarf fringe dangled lower than the wrinkled skirt that undulated around the painter's knees. The dress was supposed to be wrinkled. That was why Helen couldn't wash it. She'd forgotten the formula. Something to do with a broomstick. No, not the riding of, as Tess so rudely suggested. Last year Helen had lost a peasant-embroidered blouse, but subsequently discovered it in a bucket of water on the back porch. The winter's thawing and freezing had made interesting alterations in the blouse and Helen had toyed with the idea of putting *Cactus Sun* out to soak this year, but she'd hated to be without it so long. Of her many costumes, this Arizona purchase was the only one she felt set her turquoise off.

"Give me a cig, someone," she said when she came to the fireplace group. Leaning over the table for Sally's cigarettes, the artist clanged her necklaces against one of Rita's creations. Helen gasped, for the turquoise; Rita, for the statue.

Helen had bought this set of jewelry right off the person of an ancient chief whom she had encountered just as he was entering Santa Fe to dispose of his heritage. Next day she'd had a nasty shock. "When I saw him there in the hotel lobby, all decked out with what I thought an identical set, I was going to call the cops. But you know what? He'd sold me his real set, but now he was passing mail-order stuff off as tribal ceremonials." Here Helen would cackle about the gullibility of tourists. "He was charging exactly what he'd charged me, and getting it, too. Can you beat it?"

Having made certain that the museum pieces were still intact, Helen said she wished Sally would change her brand of cigarettes. "Golly, Sal, you should have got those invites out a month before the show," she said after she had lighted the cigarette that she complained tasted of hemp.

"Three weeks is considered proper for wedding invitations," said Sally, but Helen reminded her of what had happened last year, when Sally had run her into a conflict. Sally didn't say what she might have said, that the conflict, a charity ball which didn't start until ten o'clock, wouldn't have had to cut into Helen's preview attendance. Women from whom Sally had been buying tickets for years had looked her right in the eye, afterward, and said how sorry they were. It would be a while before some of those women would get invited to Sally Cutter's for lunch and bridge, and a long time before she would feel she had to suffer through music recitals in which certain children were appearing. She had not crossed any names off of Helen's preview list, though; she couldn't afford to do that.

"I thought it was nice not to have such a crowd," said Rita.

"There's no conflict this time," said Sally. "I checked with the papers, clubs, churches, everything. There's a travel talk at the Elks Club but we don't have any Elks on our list."

"I hope you aren't being snobbish," said Rita, "but I know you can't help the way you were brought up. Helen, we're playing a guessing game."

Helen had seated herself on the pillow stuffed into a hole the late Skip, sister of Hop and Jump, had dug in the davenport across from the sofa where Sally was sitting. The hole, even with the pillow, was deep enough and Helen's leg-swinging wide enough to reveal cotton knit underwear that was gray and torn. "Shoot," said Helen. "Get it over with."

"You're to guess whom Sally met at the parsonage on Monday," said Rita.

"Her Waterloo," said Helen.

Rita pressed a hand over her lips and then, having done with her giggles, turned to scold Tess for giving the game away.

"The Second Coming?" asked Helen.

Rita was convulsed, but she managed to tell Helen that direct questions weren't permitted yet. "The person is someone we knew in Potty's time."

"Listen," said Helen, "we had Potty fourteen years."

"Fifteen," said Rita.

"Fourteen," said Helen and demanded that George settle the question. Where was the dog book, anyway? Had anyone seen it since the Professor's death?

George said as soon as the initial work, the sorting and so on, was done, he would get busy on his father's papers. Everybody looked at Sally. The discussion about preparing the Professor's papers and books for the job that would require more skill was a debate that had been going on several years, but Sally interrupted it now by screaming. Things, frequently things propelled by more than gravity, sometimes dropped from the blackened beams, but even as she was screaming she knew Laura's cold fingers were what had brushed the back of her neck. "Laura," she said, "I wish you wouldn't sneak up behind me like that."

"Sneak?" asked Laura. "You must have something on your conscience, dear. Can I help it if I'm naturally light on my feet?"

"You could stop wearing gum soles," said Tess.

Laura came around to the coffee table for a cigarette. After putting in her complaint about the brand, she said she liked sensible clothing. "And not being a professional beauty, I can afford to be comfortable, thank God. I trust you can relax after you've got your man, Tess. It must be a frightful strain."

Laura was wearing what might have been the oldest and clumsiest of her tweeds. Her shirt, a man's, wasn't clean, because, of course, Laura was too sensible to spend a clean shirt on the family. "Or is Dr. Kildare coming here?" she asked. "From the way you're decked out . . . "

"Washing's a silly habit I've got into," said Tess.

"Children," said Rita, "stop teasing. Laura, we're playing a guessing game. Here are the clues so far . . ."

Had Laura come directly from upstairs into the studio, Sally would have seen her. Laura must have been in the study the whole time, but if Laura wanted to win games by cheating, Sally didn't care.

"With or without wings?" asked Laura when the parsonage clue was mentioned.

"Dear, as I've always said, you do not have your father's touch," said Rita, "and so why try? It's a person we knew in Potty's time, but Sally claims she never heard of the person until Monday. Of course that's silly and shouldn't be taken as a real clue."

"I'll give you a sillier clue," said George. "Laura, believe it or not, the person couldn't think of Tom's name."

"Tom Who?" Laura tugged at her necktie although it was already tied into a hard knot. She was an expert at knots and braids, but after her coronet had been up a while, little curls began to escape to remind you there was a time when Laura Cutter might have been halfway pretty, if she had tried. She was a modified version of Helen, not quite so tall, not so angular, not so thin, and her nose wasn't quite so large as Helen's. Had Tommy Gregg thought her pretty?

"Who do you think you're kidding?" asked Helen. "But where does Tom come in?"

"Not at all," said George, "according to the person."

"That's right," said Helen. "Make it good and easy. Tommy's a clue because he doesn't have anything to do with it."

"As a matter of fact, Tommy is a clue," said Rita, "but they didn't tell me and I guessed without him."

"Say!" said Helen. "I wonder how old May is."

"Fifty-three, I believe," said George.

"And you're always saying you can't guess," said Rita. "Helen, you did very well."

"Oh, for God's sake," said Helen, "is old May the answer? George, I bet she's more than fifty-three. What was she doing at the parsonage? Repenting her sins?"

"She seems unaware of having any to repent," said George. "Strange, isn't it, Laura?"

Laura, teetering on a ruined hassock, said she had no idea whom they were talking about.

"Wake up," said Helen. "May Tabor's the answer."

"May Johnson now," said Sally.

"So she finally got a man, did she?" Helen looked at her sister. "You know, Laura, I bet this proves what I always said. I never did swallow that yarn of yours about her and Tom and I think this proves it was a lot of hooey. I always knew May was nobody's fool and once burned—oops!" Now Helen looked at Sally. "Skip that last, Sal. Didn't mean a thing."

"I always liked May," said Rita. "I hope she'll come to call."

"I asked her to the preview," said Sally. "Her husband should be here by then, too."

"May Tabor is never to set foot in this house again," said Laura. "I suppose I can't prevent her from going to the art school, but I certainly can absent myself."

"Oh, Laura, let bygones be bygones," said Rita. "And I think Helen's probably right. If Tommy had wanted to marry you, I'm sure he would have. Surely we can talk about it now, dear, but you must have known then that there was no need for him to go off to Columbia. We have a very fine department of anthropology. You know the Professor always said so, and he was very critical."

"You can't by any chance be under the fantastic delusion that I would have married Tommy Gregg, can you?" asked Laura. She would have done better not to reach for another cigarette until she'd got her hands under control. Her voice was doing fairly well, but her hands were trembling and her face was twitching; Sally couldn't help feeling sorry for her. "Don't make me laugh, Rita. Why, I would have died before I would have married such a despicable . . ."

"Well, you didn't have to die or marry him, either one," said Rita, "and so why raise such a fuss? Seems like we could talk about it by now without you going into one of your tantrums. It was probably just your imagination anyhow."

"What, pray?" asked Laura. "Do tell me what I imagined, and perhaps I can fill in a few gaps."

"Tommy and May living together in New York," said Rita. "I never did believe it, but even if it was true, who could possibly care now?"

"Mr. Johnson, perhaps," said Laura. "Or was it Peterson?"

"Laura, you know May wouldn't have married that sort of person," said Rita. "Why, she wouldn't even marry George, would she, George?"

"The evidence so indicates," said George.

"Dear, you don't have to be embarrassed about it," said Rita. "You were reared in such a hidebound community that you couldn't help but pick up a little of it. And you're so much more conservative than you used to be. I hope you don't mind my saying that, Sally. You know I don't mean it unkindly."

"Oh, Sally's not so conventional as all that," said George.

"Well, now, you see, Laura? It's a matter of give and take all the way around," said Rita. "Let's have another guessing game."

"By all means," said Laura. "George, does Ann know May's come?"

"Should she?" asked George.

"I'm asking the questions," said Laura, "but maybe we shouldn't put too great a strain on Sally."

"It was damn sporting of you not to guess the answer to the first game, Aunt Laura," said Tess. "Because of course you'd heard us talking. I saw you in the study."

Laura's laughter was easy and loud. "My poor child," she said, "do you think I've nothing better to do with my time? I've been writing. Would you care to have me read the poem I've been working on this morning?"

"I've a guessing game," said Helen. "What's for chow? I called the grocery yesterday and told him to send over a flock of stuff, relatives coming, I said, and he says how about a nice sirloin and I said, Mister, when I order steak from you you'll know I'm hearing wedding bells. Look, I said, the boy we're after isn't coming and anyhow I'm not giving him steak until I'm damn sure he's signed on the dotted line. Not that I don't love you, Tess, but you know what steak is these days."

"I wish Jack had come," said Rita. "I'm thinking of doing his head. Such a fine head but, Tess, don't you get tired of germs all the time?"

"We're in surgery," said Tess. "Any of you girls like a hysterectomy cheap?"

"There are times when I begin to feel my age," said Rita. "Sometimes I feel I don't keep up. We ought to have more young people in so I can get used to how they talk."

"That's okay by me," said Helen, "if you don't ask them to stay for the eats. Sal, I didn't unwrap anything. I wouldn't take a chance like that, not with the Cordon Bleu coming."

"The which?" asked George.

"The people who never wash their omelette pans," said Helen.

"I've known them for years," said George, "but this is the first time I'd heard that they limited it to the omelette pans." He smiled at Sally.

George did notice things. He did appreciate his wife's clean kitchen and her good cooking. Oh, she had got him farther from his family than they realized. They could make fun of Sally's way, call it conservative and conventional, but George liked it. His smile said so and it made Sally less resentful about dinner.

About a year ago, goaded on by Tess, Sally announced, one Sunday when they came to this huge log house that the Professor had designed so many years ago, that she didn't feel like cooking a meal. Helen and Laura and Rita had been astounded. It wasn't that they couldn't understand why a person wouldn't feel like cooking; none of them had ever felt like it. But it just didn't sound like their little Sal. However, if Sally wanted to go temperamental on them, all right, they would go out. Helen said it would be her party. She and Rita squabbled over this, but Helen won.

And when it came time to pay the check? Son of a gun,

Helen didn't have any money on her, could you tie that? Rita could. If Laura had money along, she wasn't saying so. Except for eating, Laura had maintained a poetic aloofness. George, after pocket searching, produced fifty-five cents. He said that would take care of the tip, and was shocked when Sally said it wouldn't. It had been such a long time since George had had to think about such things; when he wasn't with Sally, he was with Ann Price.

Brad had had a quarter. Tess had said she was loaded, but damned if she'd pay for Aunt Helen's party. This had offended Helen. "As if I wasn't going to pay your mother back," she'd said.

Of course Helen had never paid Sally back. You couldn't expect an artist to remember such an inartistic detail, but Helen did remember that she'd taken the gang out. "Remember that time I took you all out to dinner?" she said now. "Boy, we sure didn't get anything like Sal puts out."

"I hope he didn't send pot roast again," said Sally. "I've told you there's nothing I can do about pot roast in a hurry."

"When Brad comes, we'll have him go out and look in the woods," said Rita. "I think some trees or branches fell during the winter and it would be nice to have a fire in the fireplace. George, do you think the woods are thinning?"

"There's bound to be some change," said George, "but there are quite a few young trees coming along."

"I don't know," said Rita. "It seemed to me we can see Sheridan Road better than we used to. The Professor wouldn't like it. I wonder if we ought to have somebody in, some tree man. But he always wanted everything left to nature. He was so fond of nature. You remember he always said this was Walden, but with plumbing."

"Well, a bow in that direction," said Tess. "Did you get the john fixed so it wouldn't run all the time?"

"Houses need humidity," said Helen. "If it's pot roast, you could grind it, Sal."

"With my teeth?" asked Sally. "That grinder doesn't work any more. I told you."

"Well, we got all day," said Helen.

"Yes, dear," said Rita. "There's no hurry. Take your time."

"I know what," said Helen. "There's a cold cut deal in the icebox, some stuff the boys didn't like, too much pepper, I guess. You fix us some of your swell little canapés and maybe I can rassle us up a drink. And then you can putter around to your heart's content and we'll never notice the time."

As Sally started to the kitchen, the two dogs lumbered after her and she heard her in-laws asking each other if that wasn't about the cutest thing they'd ever seen.

Seventeen

AS LAURA CUTTER had so succintly phrased it, there was publicity and publicity. Her brother had said this, too, and often. If publicity concerned works of art or intellect, it was public service. If it concerned something like washing machines, it was advertising of the most vulgar sort, and an attempt to rook the public.

The publicity stunt Sally's mother was currently engaged in had nothing to do with C. J. Bradford's business, but Sally was sure George would think there was a connection, and so she was hoping to keep the Mother's Day feature a secret from him. Every time a member of her family was mentioned in a newspaper, George suspected a tie-in with paid advertising. He knew that C.J. had not backed Mimi's political campaign, but along with C.J. had assumed that Mimi had learned her lesson and got her political wings clipped too close to the bone for regrowth.

"Tell George what you like," Mimi had said when issuing an invitation that had been a royal command, "but don't you dare tell him why or let him come early."

"But I didn't believe you when you said it was just a treat for Granny," said Sally. "I couldn't believe she'd be so thrilled about a feature on the four Sarahs and I don't think George is going to believe it, either."

Mimi said to tell George it was C.J.'s way of getting some free advertising. "I don't care what you tell him, so long as you don't let him know I'm going to run again," she said. "It's not to be announced until later on. And I don't want him here until the newspaper people have left. We don't want another camera fracas."

Sally's mother had been referring to the smashing of a camera several years ago. The *Chicago Daily Courier* hadn't sponsored Mrs. C. J. Bradford, but one of its photographers had crossed the barrier long enough to cause an incident. The *Courier*, perhaps with some thought about the Bradford washing-machine account, had not blamed Mrs. Bradford personally. Indeed, the paper had stated several times that she was a woman of good intentions. But it was an independent paper, and had risked C.J.'s good will by saying that Mrs. Bradford was a tool of gangster and communist elements. C.J., who never differed with the *Courier*, had been most unhappy about the entire project.

As Mimi had said, announcement of her candidacy would be premature at this time, but Tess refused to accept the Mother's Day feature plan as being something originated either by the newspaper or by her great-grandmother. "I bet Mimi's going to run for office again," said Tess. "Dr. Russak won't like it."

"He's not the only one," said Sally. "The *Courier* wouldn't run this feature if they thought Mimi still had political ideas. She fixed it so they don't know the suggestion came from her. And you can see that a nice homey story will do her a lot of good, politically."

Tess said she could see this so clearly that she couldn't agree that her father would be so stupid as to miss it. Again Sally said the idea was not to let George know about the interview until after it was over. Keeping things from Daddy wasn't so hard, she said.

And it would have been very simple, if Brad hadn't misunderstood when he was to start having the car on Saturday. George was in his study, of course. He looked up long enough to grunt when Sally said Brad or someone would pick him up a little before six-thirty. If she had had any idea that she and Tess would have to come back to the house, Sally would have closed the study door. But George probably would have heard them calling for a cab. There were two things George and his people were very careful about; one was long-distance telephoning and the other was taxicabs. If it was long distance, all the Cutters had to say hello; if it was a cab, everybody had to go along, to make it worth while.

Before Tess put the phone back on its cradle, George came tearing into the hall to say he'd have his shirt changed in two seconds. No, he wouldn't wait until someone came for him later. That would be silly, with a cab on the way. When Sally said there was no need for him to stop his work this early, he said he hadn't been able to accomplish anything, the way she and Tess had been storming around.

In the cab Tess said it would be better to tell him now and

get it over. Quickly, to prevent Tess from giving political hints, Sally spoke of her grandmother's interest in Mother's Day and of how nice it was to have four Sarahs in the family. "Four generations, George. Things like that, pictures in the paper and so on, mean a lot to an old lady who can't get out much any more, and so Mimi said the *Courier* people could come and . . ."

George acted awful. While he gave his opinion of Mother's Day in general and the *Chicago Daily Courier* in particular, it looked as if the Cutters might have to walk the rest of the way. The driver made it plain he didn't care for George's attitude, but he did deliver him to the Bradford address. "In my position," he said while Sally stayed behind to pay, "you get to see a lot of human nature. I figure it's a guilt complex with a lot of these guys." He looked at the Bradford house. "Yes, once these rich guys get a couple under their belt, it comes out."

This section of town wasn't what it had been before the opening of the new subdivisions, but its deterioration wasn't very noticeable as yet. The neighborhood was zoned against rooming houses. Fearful of being turned in by neighbors whose guests were limited to the nonpaying, the rooming-house operators kept their places up quite well. The street still looked good enough to impress people like Jack Russak and to draw Helen Cutter's description, snazzy. When Helen wished to convey appreciation of the Bradford culture, she would say their house was snah-zay.

The house was as out of fashion as Helen's slang and, like so much of Helen's vocabulary, was of a period unlikely to be revived, although Sally reminded herself that the Charleston had been revived, and that one shouldn't be too optimistic. The Bradford house, however, was more of the Bunny Hug era. It was a yellow-brick monstrosity with stone-framed plate-glass windows. The front stoop was protected by a green tiled canopy and was flanked by large cement bowls that rested on the backs of stone griffons. The bowls were filled with their winter bouquets just now.

When the weather warmed up, Kenneth, the house and yard man, would replace the evergreen with petunias, geraniums, ageratum and trailing vines. Come spring, Kenneth would rescallop his hedges, globe and cube his smaller trees and bushes and set out his cannas and elephant ears. It would have been too bad if C.J. and Mimi Bradford had objected violently to Kenneth's geometrical landscaping, because Granny Graham liked the way Kenneth did. And she liked the way Kenneth's wife, Julia, did. Granny was not the owner, but she was the boss of this house.

When Julia opened the door she quickly dropped her smile of welcome. "The paper hasn't come yet," she said.

"Should we wait outside?" asked George, but Mimi, hurrying into the hall, was exclaiming that George wasn't supposed to be here at all.

"Brad went off with the car," said Sally. "So George came along with us. I've told him it's a Mother's Day feature."

Mimi looked relieved, but she turned to C.J., who was at the library door, to suggest that he and George have a nice chat until dinner.

"Now, Mimi," said C.J. "George is going to behave. George,

you will please bear in mind that you weren't invited until six-thirty."

Sally looked hard at the nodding Julia, but you could no more stare Julia down than you could stare down her teacher, the wisp of woman seated in the living room's wide curving bay that overlooked the rose garden.

Old Mrs. Graham's hair was scraped back so tightly that she'd got an oriental lift to the corners of her pale eyes. On top of the peeled head was a flat ivory coil secured by unnecessarily stout pins. The story of Granny's beauty had passed into legend before Sally's time. Vaguely she remembered when her grandmother had been muffin-plump; she remembered when today's taffeta had been blacker and when the straps of the gunmetal kid slippers had cut into puffy feet, but she remembered none of the beauty her mother sometimes mentioned.

"A pity you girls couldn't of fixed yourselfs up to have your picture took," said Granny after they had told her how lovely she looked. As her rasping voice gave the old lady's opinion of wool suits, the bluish fingers picked at the blue and gray cameo that fastened her lace collar. This was the pin she said Adam Levering gave her because the blue matched her eyes. George said whatever your position on Levering's poetry, you could not accuse the man of having been so color blind as all that. George had frequently to be reminded of Granny's age. He was inclined to treat everybody alike. He expected babies to understand long words and he demanded reasonableness of the elderly. He no longer gave Granny any credit for his marriage. This was one old joke he didn't care for any more.

Laura Cutter had made it possible for Sally and George to

meet, but Granny had provided the igniting spark. Groping for something to say to her silent escort, Sally had asked if he cared for the works of Adam Levering. It had seemed an odd question to shout but as George had been walking three or four feet ahead of her, she'd had either to yell or say nothing. It had always been difficult for Sally Bradford to say nothing.

During that Sunday night's session she'd heard Levering's name and had wanted to put in her small oar, but then she had been struck by unique stage fright. The first time she was at the log house, one of the guests asked what she did. Sally said she went to school. "Yes," said the person who dressed like a man and spoke like a woman, "but what do you do?" Thinking he meant Activities, Sally told him what was going on at Northwestern. The man had stared at her and said, "You say you are Laura's friend?"

When she asked George about Adam Levering, he permitted her to catch up with him. "I didn't know you'd read my thesis," he said.

Knowing nothing of his thesis, not even of its existence, she said her family had always been quite interested in Adam Levering, on account of knowing him so well. Snorting, George said she must mean some other Levering. *The* Adam Levering had been dead many years before she was born. "And he left no heirs, not even a remote cousin," said George. "I've studied the matter rather intensively."

"I didn't mean *I* knew him," said Sally, "but he lived next door to my grandparents in Peters Corners, Indiana, and . . ."

"My dear young woman," said George, "it is not necessary

to give the state when you are speaking of that mecca of the nineteenth century."

"Anyhow," said Sally, "my grandmother knew him very well. He used to smoke his cigar in her parlor. His wife wouldn't let him, on account of her lace curtains."

George didn't admit it, but Sally could tell he hadn't known about Mrs. Levering's lace curtains. He was sarcastic about saying he should have put this valuable information into his thesis, but all the same he asked questions and finally he said he would like to meet Sally's grandmother.

When Sally told C.J. and Mimi that she and George were going to get married, she said George was just wanting an excuse to force an acquaintance with Granny. Granny hadn't been very cordial to him. You could not satisfy old Mrs. Graham. If they were rich, she said they were gangsters. She said George Cutter had had too much book-learning to ever amount to a hill of beans. She said George would be as good for nothing as his father and that there was something decidedly wrong with folks who would build a log house in this day and age. In the next breath, Granny would say there was something wrong with folks who used washing machines instead of good old elbow grease. You could not pin Granny down. George tried. He tried for ten or more years.

He thought he would do a definitive biography of Adam Levering. There had been a half-dozen biographies of the man but so far, said George, not the definitive one. Levering had been famous during his lifetime, but Peters Corners hadn't really been much of a mecca and little had been published about his personal life. George had drawn some conclusions about Levering's work that he wished to bolster up with information from Madam Graham. Granny was full of information, but she kept changing it around. Uncle James could reassure George on only the basic facts: Levering had lived next door to the Grahams, Uncle James remembered the beard, he remembered getting his face slapped by Edith Levering and, yes, he remembered the smell of cigar smoke in the Graham parlor and perhaps he remembered that the Levering parlor had lace curtains. Uncle James could not say positively that Levering had given Granny the cameo, but he remembered that his mother's eyes used to be bluer. "They were never so dark as Mimi's and mine," he said, "but I imagine they were as blue as the pin."

As George finally said, he didn't have much to add to what had already been written about Adam Levering. Deciding that the earlier biographers had done about as well as could be expected, George washed his hands of Levering and of Granny. He was not among the group paying court to the old woman this afternoon.

"Mimi, are you sure you got the time right?" asked C.J. He was a brisk, small-boned man whose shoes, fingernails and spectacles were always gleaming. His neatness was so dominant that one was inclined to overlook the fact that he was rather handsome. He looked about ten years younger than he was and appeared to be in excellent health, which he was not. He had a bad heart that required him to take mid-morning and mid-afternoon rests at the office, but nobody was supposed to know this or to know that personal preference was not what had made C. J. Bradford discontinue his former hobby, trout fishing in mountain streams.

When George saw photographs of C.J. in fishing togs, he roared about the resemblance to Calvin Coolidge, but it wouldn't have hurt George to copy a little of C.J.'s meticulousness. It was hard to believe that George's shirt had been fresh only a half-hour ago, and that the knot of his tie had been nearly centered. George was a wiggler. That was how he got his exercise. He hadn't an ounce of fat on him, even though he had an enormous, absent-minded sort of appetite. He told Tess that an active brain was far more effective in keeping the weight down than any noncalory diet could be.

His hair was thinning on top and his barber, presumably hoping to drape the bald spot, had let one section of the side hair grow quite long. George seemed to think this special tuft was a fingering piece. His hair was the crimped wire sort of natural curl. Just after he had used his comb, the long section of his hair was a duck-tail for the rear view, but in a moment it was moved to its more usual position out over the right ear. Now as his in-laws argued politely about which was likely to be correct about the time of an appointment, the *Chicago Daily Courier* or Mrs. C. J. Bradford, George pulled at his jutting lock and displayed labored interest.

Mimi, second Sarah of this clan, was wearing a bottle-green silk Sally hadn't seen before. So far there had been no real opportunity to comment on the dress, and Sally hoped none would develop. Like George, Mimi abandoned herself to professionals. Mrs. Bradford's clothes were expensive, but that didn't mean they fit her. Indeed, in Brentwood, the more one paid, the less likely one was to be fitted. Mimi's dressmaker, who served only the better classes, could have had success among crowned heads. Miss Vance was a wizard at using quantities of costly materials; she could guarantee that although your shoulders might sag, the rest of you would be untouched. Sally's had been a Vance wedding. Her wedding gown was still in existence, but more hidden than saved.

The problem of how to use extra amounts of green silk for the new afternoon dress had been solved by a great fan of accordion pleating that, after whirling around to pin-wheel a screen for the subject's stomach, overlapped the skirt in generous wings. It was a terrible dress, but Sally couldn't be certain that Mimi did not know this. Mimi had a politician's eye and knew that voters were leery of chic women who ran on Home and Family platforms.

"I have on my nice lace collar," said Granny, naturally bored with the conversation that had left her.

"It's good to see it again," said Sally. "You haven't worn it for a while."

"I keep my things nice," said Granny. "I wrap my lace in black tissue paper, what you'd ought to done with that shirt-waist."

Sally said her blouse was supposed to be cream-colored, but Granny paid no attention. She said Mimi had worn the lace collar for her wedding. Sally remarked that she had worn it for her wedding, and then shook her head at Tess, who was muttering something about a future bride.

"Some folks might believe I'd let a wild Indian pull my nice collar every whichaway," said Granny, "if they didn't know me. My mother wore this collar for her wedding and then she put it in black paper and saved it for me."

This was not true. The collar had been bought for Mimi's wedding, but when Granny liked something she gave away it usually came back into her possession. The handkerchief she was using this afternoon was one she had given Sally for Christmas.

The doorbell rang. "You keep an eye on George, C.J.," said Mimi, "and take him off to the library if he says anything, or looks like he's going to."

"George, whatever become of that there book you was going to write about Mr. Levering?" asked Granny.

"Mama," said Mimi, "I think the newspaper people are here."

"What newspaper people?" asked Granny. "Don't ask them to stay for supper."

Eighteen

THE BOOMING VOICE IN the reception hall told them they had been mistaken in thinking the newspaper people had come. Tess said she'd known Uncle James would manage to get into the act. "Now, Tess," said Mimi. "Uncle James has had so much experience with the press. I told him to come early if he could."

"Catherine and James managed to get here early after all," said C.J. as he ushered the James Fenimore Grahams in.

"I always like to see a picture show from the beginning," said Uncle James. After kissing his mother, he extended hearty greetings to the others. George, who had gone to a window, was studying the rose garden. He did not turn around, but Sally didn't care; Uncle James was used to George and Aunt Catherine was offended, no matter what people did.

"You poor old soul," Aunt Catherine said to Granny. "I can't understand why Mimi would subject you to such an ordeal."

"Putting on a little fat, ain't you, Cathy?" asked Granny. "Eating candy, I reckon, laying around and eating . . ."

"Yes," said Uncle James, "I wanted to be present. I've had quite a few dealings with the press."

Aunt Catherine said Mimi had had some, too.

"That's all in the past, Catherine," said C.J. "And it was just a misunderstanding."

Aunt Catherine laughed. She dated back to the school which held that a lady never used any but the upper registers of the voice. Aunt Catherine never spoke or laughed loudly, but she had a penetrating soprano that reminded her niece of the months when Billy Bradford had studied violin. "And just what did that little misunderstanding cost you, C.J.?" asked Aunt Catherine when she had done with her laughter.

"You'll split them seams," said Granny. "They're a-pulling out. I can see it from here."

Tess whispered to her mother that when Miss Vance sewed for the clerical discount, she cut cloth corners. Aunt Catherine said she was wasting away to skin and bone. The recital of what the current doctor said about how she must force herself to eat was interrupted by her husband. Uncle James said the newspaper people would be arriving any minute and that he wished to check on a few details. He said the paper would want a few words of special identification for each Sarah, something brief and to the point, for captions. "For Mama," he said, "it will be *nonagenarian who . . .*"

"I don't know as I like your language, James," said Granny.

"*. . . who is still active in the management of one of Brentwood's most charming homes,*" said Uncle James.

"Brief, to the point and certainly simple," said George.

"I never get me a minute's rest," said Granny, "what with the way my daughter gads."

"Sarah Two, prominent club leader, active in the city's most worthwhile civic enterprises," said Uncle James.

"Even snappier," said George, but they had all learned years ago that often it was wiser to ignore him.

Mimi handed Uncle James a piece of paper. "I prepared a list for them," she said.

"Just so there's nothing political," said Uncle James.

"She's dropped all that sort of thing," said C.J.

Uncle James looked over the top of his glasses but said nothing until he had read Mimi's list. "In general very good," he said, "but I would question the advisability of mentioning the Home for Unwed Mothers. Perhaps you didn't see the editorial the *Courier* had the other day on the distribution of relief funds."

"Some of those dreadful creatures are receiving as much as two hundred dollars a month," said Aunt Catherine.

"I saw the editorial," said Mimi. "I wonder why they didn't make any suggestions for alternatives, such as prison for the mothers and drowning for the offspring. But take it off if you want to."

"Fortunately it's at the top," said Uncle James as he tore the paper. "It's a matter of expediency, my dear."

Had Mimi told him her secret? But the expression on her mother's face made Sally conclude that Uncle James had not been informed of the ulterior motive. Uncle James simply had guessed. As Sally had often told George, a man who associated with people learned a great deal about human nature. Cab drivers? But couldn't George see that first-hand association was as important as what one learned from books? The trouble was that most of the persons George would have liked to associate with were long dead. Why, then, did he refuse to embrace Uncle James's hope of heaven? Why did he laugh when Sally said maybe in another world he would learn the true facts about Adam Levering from Levering himself? Did he laugh only because she said *true* facts? "If you would read the newspapers more carefully," she had told him in defense of the mistake she hadn't meant to make, "you would know there are many gradations of facts these days."

Tess's identification had been disposed of; her job was a fact the family accepted in the belief that it couldn't last and that commercial pictures never looked like real people anyhow. Uncle James asked if they might add that she was engaged to Dr. John Russak, presently interning at the North Shore Hospital, but he didn't argue when Tess said no. "Now for Sally," he said. The problem child had been left for last. How were they to identify Sarah Three? Uncle James said of course they could say Sally was active in organizations similar to those in which her mother . . . "I belong to everything," said Sally, "but you know I'm not active that way. I'm not a chairman of anything this year."

"She was captain of the hockey team at high school," said George.

"How about a hobby?" asked Uncle James.

"I've been asked to exhibit some of my laces at the church next Wednesday," said Aunt Catherine from the remote chair she'd gone to when Uncle James had interrupted her. "But

I must check the insurance policy first, to see if it holds if the collection is taken over to the church."

"You still play the piano, don't you?" asked Uncle James.

"She knows 'The Happy Farmer' by heart," said Tess.

C.J. said he estimated that this had cost him several thousand dollars. "But will she play it for me?"

"Say I'm a devotee of *la cuisine*," said Sally.

"Herbs are popular just now," said Mimi, "but I think they make things taste like medicine."

"I would like me a good hot cup of sassafras tea," said Granny, "now it's coming on spring."

Again Aunt Catherine's attempt to present medical information was interrupted, this time by the doorbell. The newspaper had arrived so promptly on the stroke of five-thirty that C.J. assumed Mimi had been mistaken about the time set for the appointment. He nodded to her. "It's an old trick," said Mimi. And it was one Sally had used: if you arrived sharply on the half-hour, the hostess could never be quite sure who had been wrong.

Moistening her lips, Sally concentrated on the word "cheese" and tried to forget that, dewy-lipped or not, she took a miserable picture. Glancing at her photogenic daughter, she saw that Tess had assumed her professional pose. The facial trademark of Tess's business was a look of weary nausea. Regurgitation, one felt, had taken place, but had not been completed. Tess had explained that the wares she exhibited were too borderline; the slightest suggestion of a smile would label the costume a practical joke, she said, and of course alienate the potential customer.

"Tess, this is one birdie you can smile for," said Sally.

"Mother, for heaven's sake, don't say *cheese* when they take the pictures," said Tess. "It makes you look so idiotic."

George, turning for a moment from his contemplation of the burlap-wound rose bushes, smiled at his wife. Would he smile when his name was mentioned in the introductions? But Sally knew better than to give last-minute instructions. During the recent holidays, on the way to a party, she had warned George not to be funny. "I mean, don't pun," she said. "People don't do it any more and most of them never did."

"But it's so hard for me to remember dirty stories," he said.

"You just keep quiet," said Sally, and George hadn't said a word until someone asked if he was ill. No, not physically ill, George had said, but he and the little woman were having trouble . . .

Yes, it was best not to tell George how to acknowledge introduction to the *Courier* men. One never knew when the Cutter humor would strike or in what form. Marriage to a man chary of his handshaking had made Sally observant and in the past few years she had been noticing that even quite nice men no longer seemed to feel required to tear across a room to shake hands. Some acknowledgment was still required, though, and she did hope George would at least grunt when his name was called.

In the bay, Granny had composed herself into a portrait. Her hands were folded in her lap, with the beautiful handkerchief held just so; her feet were toed out on her little footstool and her eyes, though faded in color, were bright in expression. Madam Graham looked as sharp as a tack, and she was.

What strangers didn't understand was that the sharpness was not limited to one tack; it was contained in a large box of separate items used individually. Granny was alert on one subject and then alert on something else. There was little continuity or repetition, but the old woman was never at loss.

Ever since she was eight years old, Sally had been making allowances for her grandmother, but now when she reminded George that Granny was over ninety and that he must make allowances, she knew that her own feeling for her grandmother had not altered. She did not like Granny. She knew it was wicked to dislike the elderly, but she was comforted by the knowledge that her grandmother did not like her. Now that Billy was dead, Granny talked about what a dear little chap he had been and how tormented by his sister. Granny recalled horrendous incidents that nobody else could remember. As George said, the stories she presented could not be used in any serious work.

But somewhere in Granny's varied tales about Adam Levering, might there be a truth that the fact-bound scholar, deep in footnotes, could not discover? Sally had asked George this question and he had come back with a barrage she had been unable to answer. When was Levering born, what was the date of his death, how many books did he publish, how many poems, essays, what was his basic philosophy? "All I know," Sally had said, "is that when Granny talks about him, I get a definite impression of a real person rather than a piece of required reading." George had said he wasn't writing for the mentally lazy housewife. He said what she wanted was romantic fiction, available at the corner drug store.

"How good of you to come," said Mimi as she rose to greet the men C.J. was bringing into the living room.

"Mighty close to supper time, if you ask me," said Granny. "Who is it, Sally?"

Nineteen

THE NEWSPAPER people Sally had encountered before were women covering club, social or church events. There was no way to single these women out; they could have been members, in some cases they were, or they could have been guests invited for purely social reasons, which they possibly sometimes were. At any rate, the newspaperwomen Sally had seen weren't different or freakish or unusual enough to give her a set idea of what a newspaper-woman looked or acted like; but without realizing it, she had accepted Hollywood and the stage as authorities on the masculine element of the world of journalism. So it was disappointing when C.J. brought in two hatless men, neither smoking, who did not talk out of the corner of the mouth and who appeared to be sober, and in no hurry to stop the presses. They said how-do-you-do and shook whatever hands were offered.

George glanced around. Aunt Catherine sniffed, but these gaucheries were lost in Uncle James's delighted recognition of Mr. Landis, his good and valued friend. Everyone remembered the square-dancing story Mr. Landis had done for Community Church? "What's all the ruckus?" asked Granny.

"Mama, may I present my good and valued friend, Mr.

Landis, the *Courier*'s ace reporter who is going to write you up?" Ignoring his mother's remark that she did not intend to go up until after her supper, Uncle James said the family was very lucky to have got Mr. Landis.

Mr. Landis, the older of the two *Courier* men, said he and Mr. Gunderson were the lucky ones. Mr. Landis had beautiful white hair. He was wearing a dark blue suit as neat as C.J.'s and his shirt was immaculate and his necktie a modest blue and gray stripe. Sally felt she had seen him somewhere before, but decided he resembled someone in the movies, somebody who played banker types.

While Granny was saying she had already given to the Community Chest and they didn't need to think they could pull the wool over her eyes by coming around again, Tess and Mr. Gunderson carried on a peculiar conversation. Tess asked the tall blond photographer if the regulars were covering a big fire. ". . . or a shooting and so they have to send the office boys out?" Mr. Gunderson said it wasn't often anybody pulled a fast one on old Landis and asked how Tess had swung this commercial.

"So you two youngsters already know each other," said Uncle James after he had explained to Granny that the *Courier* men weren't seeking pledges for the Community Chest.

"I'll thank you to take your hands off that lamp," said Granny to Mr. Gunderson.

"Go ahead and move anything you like, gentlemen," said C.J. "Granny, these gentlemen want to take your picture."

"They don't have to tear the house down, do they?" asked

Granny. "Anyways, Clarence, I don't know as I want my picture took." Under the false impression that C.J. disliked his given name, she made a special point of calling him Clarence when strangers were present. "Young man, this lace collar come from England in seventeen sixty-one."

There was a rustle from the end of the room where the lace expert sat, but the newspapermen were concentrating on the bay group. Mimi looked questioningly at her brother, but Uncle James just tapped his nose. He did, however, speak up when Granny answered one of Mr. Landis' later questions by saying she didn't know if she had more than the two children living.

"My brother Andrew resides in Philadelphia," said Uncle James. "I fancy he inspired the term, Philadelphia lawyer." Now the wordless but audible exception was taken by the word-custodian at the far window, but Uncle James was accustomed to speaking through coughs, sneezes, baby-squalling and snores and his rhythm never faltered. When he had finished with repeating that his brother Andrew was a Philadelphia lawyer, he tapped his nose. This time the gesture meant they could laugh.

"Dead and buried for all we know," said Granny.

Mr. Landis stopped smiling. He had undoubtedly been told that this family was just right for Mother's Day and here, from what Granny said, was something that looked as if it might shape into a skeleton in the closet. Quickly Uncle James informed the reporter that Andrew Graham wrote to his mother every Sunday of the year.

"This is Saturday," said Granny. "It don't take a week to kill and bury a man."

Mr. Gunderson, whose duties seemed to require him to hover around Tess, said he felt he was beginning to get some insight into her character. Tess said less emphasis on the feeling, please.

"My brother Andrew is older than I am," said Uncle James. "My sister, of course, is my junior. But Andrew is still in active practice."

"Anything to get out of the house," said Granny. "My boys never had a grain of sense when it come to women."

"And let us hope my sister and I also take after our dear mother in the matter of longevity," said Uncle James. "I regret to say that our father passed from this mortal sphere before reaching sixty."

"Seventy the day before he died," said Granny. "The party killed him. I knowed it would and said so, but would she listen?"

By now Mr. Landis had caught on that he wasn't to consider Madam Graham a source. He smiled at her, but except for the information about the collar, he hadn't written down anything she'd said. He really was a most attractive man, and not nearly so old as Sally had thought at first. He might be no older than George.

"But Edith would have the party and so I baked the cake," said Granny. "Hers warn't fit to eat. I done what I could for the poor man. I tell you he was so bad took he couldn't hardly move, but a lot she cared."

"As usual my mother's mind moves far more rapidly than

mine," said Uncle James, "and she has a true gift for what constitutes a story. Mama, I'm glad you mentioned the Leverings. This little sidelight . . ."

"Ladies," said Mr. Gunderson, "if we could all look at the Reverend for this one. Reverend, maybe you'll have to say something funny, but not too funny."

"The assignment could be handled more competently by Dr. Cutter," said Uncle James.

"That did it, Reverend," said the photographer, and again explained to Granny that he wasn't playing with a chemical set.

"As I was saying," said Uncle James, "this little sidelight might be of interest to your readers. Back in Peters Corners, an Indiana hamlet that will long be revered because of Adam Levering, the family lived next door to the great sage and poet. I am sure you gentlemen are familiar with Adam Levering's work."

The gentlemen weren't saying, but that was all right, the Reverend would do the talking. He covered the essays and then, with a glance at George, took up the poems. "Toward the end of his life, Levering produced what I consider the greatest of our religious poetry. Some of our finest hymns . . ."

"A heathen from the word go," said Granny. "Mr. Levering never set foot in a church."

"This time, ladies . . . wait a sec." Arranging the next pose obliged Mr. Gunderson to come over to Tess again. Sally tried not to listen, but was unable to avoid hearing her daughter ask if being a masseur wouldn't give Mr. Gunderson more scope for his natural talents. Mr. Gunderson said something about the pill-pusher, but fortunately Uncle James could top anybody's volume.

The minister said it scarcely behooved him to commend failure to join forces with organized religion, but that he harbored no doubt about Adam Levering's spiritual dedication. Again he was endangering the smooth progress of the interview. Whether Adam Levering was inspired or obsessed and in either case, by what, was a bone the Doctors Graham and Cutter had been growling over for years. The Bradfords exchanged nervous looks. Dr. Cutter glared in this direction, but turned away when his wife shook her head.

"No, no, Mrs. Cutter," said Mr. Gunderson, back at his camera. "As we were, please. Now, if we would all look at Mrs. Graham, as if we were listening to a story? Mrs. Graham, if you would make like telling a story?"

Make like? Granny *was* telling a story. She was telling about Edith Levering's lace curtains and how Mr. Levering couldn't smoke his cigar at home. "Not that he minded the excuse to come over to my place," said Granny. "That woman, why, his first wife wasn't cold in her grave before Edith moved in. He thought she was a hired girl sent by his friends. He told me so himself and I told George for his book that he couldn't get published. It was the scandal of the town when I was still a little girl. . . ."

Mr. Gunderson was so pleased with the story-hour pose that he took several shots of it.

"I was just a little shaver when Adam Levering passed away," said Uncle James, "but I well remember that noble visage."

"Handsomest man I ever did see," said Granny. "It's a crying shame Mimi can't recollect her father. She wasn't but three when he died."

"Why, Mama, I was a grown woman," said Mimi.

"Give you that green name, he did," said Granny. "Said you was the prettiest baby he ever did see. I humored him, poor man, and after a while everybody was a-saying Mimi. She'd ought to growed out of it, but Clarence here thought it was cute, I reckon. . . ." On and on, but finally Mr. Landis had a chance to say he would like to run over his information. Could he have a little more on Mrs. Cutter?

"Our daughter has an interesting hobby," said C.J. "Horticulture."

"Yes, yes," said Uncle James, almost as enthusiastically as he would have spoken had he thought of this hobby himself. "It's too bad you can't get a picture of her charming garden."

"There's always the conservtry," said Tess and from the quick glance Mr. Landis gave the girl, Sally deduced that he might have a daughter of his own.

"I often wondered what became of you," he said to Sally when he came over to say good-bye.

Hoping to delay or avoid admission that she could not place him, Sally said it had been ages since anyone had said that to her. "They always used to, when the Sally songs were still popular," she said, and then remembered a boy playing a piano. "Say! What color was your hair?"

"I'll never get used to that question," he said. "I had the reddest . . ."

"Red Landis, of course!" she said. "You're a Sigma Nu. I

don't know what possessed me not to know you right away." No older than George? He had been in Sally's class at the University. Every time Sally had gone to the Sigma Nu house, Red Landis had played all the Sally songs. Of course he might have played them anyhow, but didn't he use to look at her quite a lot? She certainly remembered those reddish brown eyes now.

Uncle James was saying how nice it was that Sally and Mr. Landis had discovered each other. "C.J., did you hear that? Mr. Landis is a Sigma Nu. . . . Mr. Landis, C.J. and I deviated. Andrew is a Sigma Nu, but we mistook an address and arrived at the Beta house."

"That reminds me I wanted to offer these gentlemen a drink," said C.J. "Now that the business is over . . ."

But Mr. Landis said unfortunately it wasn't over, that he and Mr. Gunderson had another appointment. However, he wasn't in too great a hurry. He asked Sally what had become of her. "I mean suddenly," he said. "I got a pledge lined up to spell me at the piano and then you stopped coming to our tea dances."

"George had already graduated," explained Mimi. "So she dropped out of campus things even before she left school." Mimi wouldn't have said this to prevent the newspaper from discovering George's barbarianism; she must have said it to keep Sally from revealing that there had been a gap between her Sigma Nu days and her engagement. As if Sally didn't have enough political sense to refrain from mentioning Tony Cado!

"Well, you certainly haven't changed," said Mr. Landis to Sally. "You look exactly like you did the last time I saw you."

Everybody but Aunt Catherine and George smiled happily. George laughed.

But Sally may have been mistaken in thinking George had been laughing at her and Mr. Landis. As soon as the family was alone, George laughed again. He said he had something he wanted to show Uncle James. "As soon as Brad comes," he said, "I'll run home and get it. It won't take a minute."

"Oh, George," said Mimi, "let's not have an evening of batting those old poems around. I saw you when James mentioned them. James, you shouldn't have. It was good of you to keep your mouth shut, George, and don't think I don't appreciate it. All the same, if you two are going to spend the evening . . ."

"I have a splitting headache already," said Aunt Catherine. "The fumes from those flash bulbs."

"I won't bother the rest of you," said George. "It's just an old picture I always meant to show Uncle James. We'll take it to the library after dinner."

"He was, for the funeral," said Granny. "Edith wouldn't have it no other way but he'd be buried from the church. Her and her airs. Go ahead, I told her. I said it would be the last she'd have to do with the poor man because she warn't a-going where he'd went, not if she set in the front pew the rest of her days. Killed him, that's what she done, and I said so, right to her face."

"Did she ever say anything to you?" asked George.

Twenty

"YOU'D OUGHT TO EAT your dinner at noon," said Granny. With a nice combination of triumph and disgust she sipped clear soup and nibbled melba toast. "Swilling like pigs," she said to the others, who were drinking broth and eating curls of dried bread. But she was right, abundance was coming and she was the only one leaving. She had told them the digestion stopped at nightfall, but had they profited from their instruction?

Defiantly she looked at Jack Russak, but Young Doctor had learned his lesson. A few months ago he had got his ears pinned back when he had belittled the therapeutic value of a sack of asafetida placed on the stomach of a voyager. Nodding recognition of Jack's surrender, Granny progressed to the secret of her success: from morning till night she had never known a moment's idleness. If C.J. had seen the washes she'd hung on her line in Peters Corners, he'd be mortified with shame at the linty gray laundry his murderous contraptions turned out. More than one woman had been scalped by them machines and more than one child had an arm tore off. . . .

"James would of laid abed till noon, if he'd had his ruthers," said Granny.

"Yes, I've always been a very good sleeper," said Uncle James.

"I don't know when I've had a full night's sleep," said Aunt Catherine.

"Try doing a little work for a change and you'll sleep," said Granny. "All you do all day long is lay around and nap and eat. First crow of the cock and out I'd hop."

"When we were in Taxco," said Mimi, "a man from New York asked if we'd heard the crows in the night."

"I declare you talk like a slum child," said Granny. "Crows don't caw in the night."

"He meant roosters," said Mimi.

"Burros make a very startling sound," said C.J.

"How very interesting," said George. "I believe I have never heard it. Could you illustrate?"

"I've no use for foreigners," said Granny. "I would hurry down to the woodshed. . . ."

Uncle James's eyebrows rose while his mother told how she had split her kindling and laid her fire. *My* pump, said his eyes while Granny primed it, *my* pails of water, *my* chapped hands. When Granny got out her washboard, Mimi's were the protesting eyes. "You don't listen to me," said Granny, as exasperated by silence as she could be by interruption, "but wait till you drop in your tracks, carousing all night when good Christians are sound asleep in their beds."

"Mimi, tell how you used to slide down the porch roof after

she'd gone to sleep," said Tess, but C.J. was asking if Granny was ready to go upstairs.

"You'd ought to be the one," said Granny. "I know the look, C.J. Mark my words, you ain't long for this world." She took no part in conspiracies. Yes, she said her mind in plain English and none of that Boston whine that sounded like a person had ought to blow her nose. "And if I was a-mind, I could tell you who'd go next after C.J."

This special attention should have pleased Aunt Catherine, who for at least thirty years had been assuring them she was at death's door, but her mother-in-law's stare seemed to infuriate her. It was amazing how red in the face the sufferer from pernicious anemia could become.

"She's going to be very disappointed if that elevator never breaks down," said C.J. when he came back to the dining room. "The latest is that I've had it fixed so it goes up to the attic first, to give her head a good bump, before it stops at the second floor."

"She flips in and out of it by herself all day long," said Mimi, but Julia, standing by to glower at the way C.J. was carving, said the elevator was jerking something awful. Madam was right, she said, to suspicion it.

Julia was no fool; she knew who paid the bills, but she knew the bill payer was not ruler of the roost. And she was smart enough to know she and Kenneth would be excused from this house when Madam Graham died. So why mind her manners?

C.J. said he would have the elevator checked. "Rare for you, Catherine?"

Aunt Catherine said the sight of rare meat made her skin crawl, but since the doctor insisted . . .

"I shouldn't have to tell you, C.J.," said Uncle James. "You surely know that Catherine and I would be more than happy to . . ."

But Aunt Catherine wasn't too absorbed in her anemia to anticipate what her husband was about to say. She finished the sentence for him and added a paragraph. Certainly they would be happy to take Granny, but unfortunately the doctor had ruled against it. Aunt Catherine had so hoped he would say that at long last she was up to it but, no, he absolutely . . . "But what about Andrew? I must say he hasn't hurt himself. I don't know why it should be just our responsibility. It's been years since he's had her come to Philadelphia."

"This is Mama's home," said Mimi. "There's no question about her ever leaving it again, even for a visit."

This wasn't strictly true. The question of whether Granny could abide staying here another minute was probably raised as often now as it had been while Billy and Sally Bradford were children. However, Granny no longer demonstrated her independence by going off to Philadelphia or over to the parsonage for a few days. It had been fifteen or sixteen years since she had packed bag and baggage, but to hear her tell it, her entire widowhood had been spent in being knocked around from pillar to post. Julia, showing them what she thought of people who would treat an old lady so abominably, held the vegetables just high enough to force them to serve themselves very awkwardly. "Look," said Brad when she came to him, "I'd just as soon omit the vitamins anyway."

Granny could have stayed in Peters Corners or she could have had a house or apartment elsewhere. C.J. had offered her anything she wanted, including a substantial income. Granny had informed him she wasn't from stock that would live on charity; she would work her way, thank you. So she came to this house to work herself to death and to give the Bradfords a clearer understanding of why Grandfather Graham had spent so little time at home. Well, Sally had never heard either of her parents say this, but she knew that Mimi felt she hadn't known her father very well. "He was a man's man," Mimi had told Sally. "He liked to fish and hunt and play cards. There was always a card game going on at the back of the store."

During the main course another wife demonstrated why another husband had been active in parish work. Repeating her blood history, Aunt Catherine accepted another serving of the beef. It was all she could do to choke food down, but this new doctor had said she must insulate her nerves and think, think about her blood. For a person too cultured to blow her nose in public, it was surprising what she would say about why she couldn't take prescription iron.

To get the conversation away from the lower bowel, Uncle James recounted some of his experiences in the First World War, in which he had served as chaplain. When he told the story about turning his head just in time to miss having it shot off, he was interrupted. Brad demanded to know why Uncle James hadn't been down on his belly. Aunt Catherine shuddered. "Such language at table," she said, and even Dr. Russak saw the humor in the woman's discrimination. At any rate the corners of his mouth twitched enough to make Sally think perhaps he wasn't hopeless, after all.

A gentle kick prevented Brad from entering the conversation again, but after he had finished his dessert, he rolled his eyes at his mother. But his grandmother remembered how it was with young people. Mimi said Brad could be excused. Jack and Tess, too, she said, but perhaps they would stay for coffee?

Politely Jack said he and Tess were free for the evening and that he could think of nothing pleasanter than spending it with Tess's family. "Our chums being on duty," said Tess. "It's got so we can't endure the trivial chatter of our other contemporaries such as models and the sort of riffraff I'm forced to associate with in *my* work."

Mimi remarked that she had noted a good deal of triviality, to say nothing of monotony, in the chatter Tess had had with the *Courier* photographer. Mimi liked Jack and lately was out of patience with Tess. Recently she had informed Sally that the offer to provide the grandest wedding Tess could wish for would be withdrawn if the young lady broke off with Jack Russak. The way Tess had been treating Jack shocked Mimi. Somehow Sally had not felt up to going into the other side of the question with her mother. She couldn't help feeling that Mimi, even though associated with wayward girls for many years, didn't know much about sex.

"I trust you still have some of that superlative brandy," said Uncle James.

"James," said Aunt Catherine, "it's Saturday night."

"And perhaps a rather special Saturday night," said Uncle

James. "Catherine, my dear, this is one time I would strongly advise you to fortify yourself."

When they went into the living room Aunt Catherine was still speaking on the depravity of alcoholics. She gave particular emphasis to the ministerial addicts, but when she received her little cup of coffee she forgot about alcohol. Suspiciously she looked at the service on the table in front of Mimi and then she announced that Julia had handed her a cup of pure caffeine. "Julia," she said, "you've taken the ribbon from my pot and now you've got them mixed up."

"I don't need no ribbon to mark what you drink," said Julia. "All I got to do is take a whiff. They do more than take something out of that stuff, they put something in. Dope, likely, so's the addicks will keep on buying it."

Twenty-one

FINALLY JULIA LEFT AND the family was gathered around Kenneth's geometrical, almost artificially well-behaved fire. Sipping the cordial she found less distasteful than her father's fine brandy, Sally thought about Red Landis and, thinking about Mr. Landis' hair, wondered if white hair would become George Cutter. George was very slow about turning gray. Needed he to sprawl in a chair quite so sloppily?

Of course Red was just wanting to be polite, when he had said that about having wished to dance with Sally, but that was all right, she liked people to say pleasant things. Why couldn't George be nicer? He meant it as a compliment, she supposed, when he told her she was very well preserved but somehow that never gave the glow she'd experienced when Red told her she hadn't changed. Had she felt a little the way that May Johnson felt when George opened the door? But, wait a minute, that was a feeling to be reserved for Tony Cado; it wasn't something one was supposed to have when meeting a person who was about the same as a total stranger. For no reason at all she began to think of what those three young women, Dot, Scootie and Barb had said at the Alliance tea. The cordial, she decided, must not be so mild as she had thought.

Uncle James was fidgeting around. With jabs of the poker, he ruined Kenneth's plan. The fire blazed up and would not last the evening. Aunt Catherine, who had taken a chair next to Tess, the better to complain about cigarette smoke, scolded her husband. "James, can't you sit down? You make me dizzy and I already have a splitting headache."

"Well, George," said Uncle James, after he had come to the love seat where Sally was sitting, "are you ready to exhibit your picture?"

"I suppose we'll all have to go to Helen Cutter's preview," said Aunt Catherine. "I was sick in bed a week after the last one. I don't know why you encourage her. She has no talent and that school is as bad as the Art Institute, but nobody around here has any taste. Tess, are you sure that's your cup?"

Tess turned the cup to show the lipstick marks and, with flourishes, Aunt Catherine removed herself to a more distant chair.

"I realize you wanted to wait until Brad left," said Uncle James. "I agree he's too young."

"He had lipstick on his face when he came in last Saturday night," said Tess. "He's coming along."

"Somebody must have played a joke on him," said Sally. "Brad isn't interested in girls yet."

"Just girl," said Tess. "I don't think Aunt Patricia's shade's the right one for Patty."

Again Uncle James asked George about a picture. George

said later on he and Uncle James might go to the library. "It's just something I meant to show you a long time ago but I forgot about it."

"No, George," said Uncle James. "One does not forget what one has not known. It is possible that in your subconscious . . ."

"Give him alcohol and he always starts talking about the subconscious," said Aunt Catherine. "It's disgusting. C.J., don't you dare give him any more of that brandy."

"I do wish you would have some before George shows us his picture," said Uncle James.

"I'm not going to pass it around," said George. "It's nothing to show in public."

Uncle James looked around the room. "Public? The newspaper has gone. We're just family."

Squirming under George's pointed gaze, Jack Russak said he remembered an errand he must do for his friend Arthur. He had Arthur's car primarily for this errand and didn't know why it had slipped his mind until now. "But everything was so pleasant, Mrs. Bradford. Tess, if you've finished your coffee . . ."

Tess told him it was a nice try. "But you aren't going to drag me away when the party's beginning to perk up," she said, "when my father is on the brink of showing dirty pictures."

"Really, George," said Aunt Catherine, "I always considered your sense of humor most juvenile, but I had hardly expected . . ."

"It's nothing but an old picture that may have some bearing

on a discussion Uncle James and I had some years ago," said George. "It wouldn't interest the rest of you."

"Then you never should have said it was something Brad's too young for," said Sally. "You gave us a definite come-on."

"It's exasperating not to be able to place a monetary wager," said Uncle James. He took a notebook and pencil from his pocket. "Catherine, couldn't you let me bet an old hat? It's a pity to pass up such a sure thing." Tilting the notebook so Sally couldn't see, he wrote something, tore out the page, folded it and passed it to George.

"We always play guessing games at the log house," said Tess.

"A confession of intellectual sterility," said Aunt Catherine. "George, give me that paper."

George unfolded the paper, glanced at it and then threw it into the fire. "All right, Uncle James," he said. "You win."

"Well," said Sally, "that was a quick one. Now what shall we play?"

But Uncle James was holding a hand out to George. After shrugging, George produced an envelope and gave it up. "From now on," he said, "it is yours. But the least you can do is to look at it before passing it around. Look at it and try to think of the consequences."

"Are you afraid of the truth?" asked Uncle James.

"I am afraid of seeming truths that cannot be proved or disproved," said George.

Uncle James took the picture from the envelope and shielded it with his hands. "What stronger proof could you want?" he asked. "It's better than I had hoped. George, there is security in the knowledge of the truth. For me it has been more than security. Yes, I have felt guilty about not sharing it, but I hadn't enough to offer. I didn't have this."

"So you have known all along," said George.

"Not *all* along," said Uncle James, "but longer than I have known you. I owe you an apology of sorts. But I still think they are rousing good hymns."

"I knew it, I knew it," said Tess. "You two certainly can go out of your way to get to your old poetry fight. Okay, Jack. The whole thing was just a new build-up for their unbearable Levering talk."

"Unbearable talk, perhaps," said Uncle James, "but, please, not unbearable Levering." He had risen. Would the others excuse him if he showed the picture to his wife first? "It doesn't concern her so intimately as it does some of the rest of us, but I've a feeling she will be more concerned, if George will permit me to make a small play upon the word. . . . As you see, my dear, the suggestion of brandy was in the nature of a prescription. I fancy you'll be taking some later, medicinally. I wished to spare you the preamble."

"James, the older you get, the longer you talk about nothing," said Aunt Catherine. She looked at the picture her husband had given her. "Well, how quaint! Gracious, you've gained a terrible amount of weight since this was taken. No wonder George thought you would want to think twice before showing it around. I suppose you were at some drunken masquerade party. Where did you get that ridiculous rig?"

"Unless my history is shakier than I'd thought," said Uncle James, "that rig was Government Issue for the Civil War."

"As if I didn't know!" said Aunt Catherine. "*My* family was very well represented in that war. Did you have a relative in it?"

"Obviously," said Uncle James.

"You could have rented it," said Aunt Catherine. "I don't see why you say a thing is obvious when it is not. You could have rented or borrowed the costume. I refrain from saying how else you could have got it."

Now all of them, except George, crowded around Aunt Catherine to exclaim how slender Uncle James had been. Tess said Jack would give Uncle James a diet that wouldn't be too difficult. Jack said yes, he would be happy to oblige. "Hold your horses," said C.J. "James was only eighteen when I met him and already pretty hefty. This fellow looks to be nearly middle-aged and, anyway, that picture was never taken in our day. It's more the vintage of my mother's album."

"Yes, it's a real Civil War soldier," said Mimi, "but who can it be?"

"It's James, all right," said Aunt Catherine. "He got an old-fashioned photograph to go with his costume, but you can't fool me, James. I know that look. Drunk as a lord. See how his eyes are popping."

"Our eyes do not pop," said Uncle James.

"It certainly does look like him," said Jack. "It's more than the eyes. The structure of the mouth and chin . . ."

"Yes," said Uncle James, "I noticed that. Mama always made so much of the eyes that I hadn't expected anything else."

Then Mimi laughed. "Well, for pity sakes," she said, "of

course it's Cousin Henry! George, how in the world did you get hold of it? Mama's always saying she never saw a picture of him. You know, she's told us so many wild tales about him that I'd got to thinking he was an invention. I wonder why she never said he was in the Civil War."

"Too dull for her," said C.J. "Granny likes Indians. Well, well, she's certainly been right about those eyes. George, did James really write Henry's name on that paper?"

"Oh, God," said George.

"No," said Uncle James, "what I wrote was '*sans* beard.'"

"Nuts," said Tess, and went back to her chair. "People couldn't get away with that kind of guessing at Rita's. *Sans* beard, *avec* beard, you stood a fifty-fifty chance of winning. More. It might have been a woman. Mother, what would that make the odds?"

But Sally mentioned that she thought there was some writing on the back of the picture and Aunt Catherine turned it over. The writing was faded but legible: "Adam Levering, home from war."

Jack said he and Tess really must go. The drug stores around here didn't stay open very late, and he didn't want to drive his friend's car any farther than necessary, because Arthur had said something was wrong with the carburetor.

And why was Jack Russak so bright all of a sudden, how come he'd been able to figure out what Sally couldn't see? But if she had not arrived at the same conclusion, how could she guess what was in Jack's mind? How dared he to think such a thing of her grandmother! Slowly she went back to the love seat.

"I didn't want you to see it, did I?" asked George. "I'm sorry I ever mentioned it, but I never thought the old fool . . ."

"I don't believe it," said Sally, "not for a minute."

George said nobody was asking her to.

"Yes, they are," said Sally. "Uncle James is and so are you, and even Jack."

"Tess," said Jack, "let's get going."

"Oh, stop it," said Sally. "It isn't as simple as that. You're in on it this far, Jack, and so sit down. Or do something about the fire. Put some more wood on it. My feet are freezing."

She looked down at her brown leather spectators but she was seeing blue satin slippers that had been ruined when she had run away from Tony Cado. Shivering, she remembered how the slush had seeped through the thin soles before she had been rescued by the complimentary cab driver. Granny, she had thought when the man commended her for being a good girl, would have been proud of her, too. Whose granny? That little old woman who fingered a blue and gray cameo, who spoke of cigars and lace curtains? Busy inventing what Granny would have said, Sally knew that for many years she hadn't noticed what her grandmother had actually said. Not just this afternoon. Granny had been saying it over and over for years, and all of the family, except Uncle James, had thought it senile inability to stay on one subject.

"I don't get it," said Tess. "What's everybody acting so funny about? Give me the picture, Aunt Catherine. Isn't it Cousin Henry?"

"Go run your errands," said George. "It has nothing to do with you."

"If Adam Levering was Uncle James's father, he was Mimi's father," said Sally. "Are you trying to say I'm not Mimi's child?"

"Are we back to Adam Levering again?" asked Tess. "Can't we ever get away from that man?"

"No," said Uncle James.

Twenty-two

WATCHING AUNT Catherine, Uncle James had been prepared for the attempt to destroy the picture. The flabby fingers had torn only a corner of the heavy cardboard before they were pried loose. "As I understand it," said Uncle James, "this is a rare literary item and hardly ours to dispose of. And would its destruction alter the truth?"

"You're the dupe of a practical joker," said Aunt Catherine. "You should know from his sister's painting and the other one's poetry, if not from the man himself. Don't you know water can be mixed with ink?"

C.J. said Catherine must not say a thing like that. He said there was some simple explanation. Did this mean, asked Mimi, that C.J. did not believe that Adam Levering was her father?

"Honestly, Mimi!" said Tess. "You people! You sound like little children."

"There must be a rational explanation," said C.J. "I think George should tell us how he came by it."

"You all know I advertised for letters, photographs, any

material that might have bearing on the subject," said George. "Perhaps four or five years after I stopped work on the biography, I received that picture from a woman who said she found it among her mother's belongings. Her mother had lived in Peters Corners, and this woman remembered hearing her speak of Levering. She had cut my notice from the *New York Times* but hadn't got around to doing anything about it until she'd taken her mother's things from storage. This photograph was in . . ."

"And you couldn't smell blackmail?" asked Aunt Catherine. "How much did she want?"

"She didn't want anything," said George. "She said she supposed I already had this picture but as she had no use for it . . ."

"Apparently she had never read the biographies," said Uncle James. "They all agree there was no early photograph in existence."

"You wait until you get her next letter," said Aunt Catherine. "Didn't you have sense enough to put it into the hands of a lawyer?"

"I never heard from her again," said George. "As I said, I was through with Levering. I just stuck the picture in my files."

"If the old woman lived in Peters Corners," said C.J., "it is quite likely she knew Cousin Henry, too."

Mimi said she saw what C.J. meant. "I've done it myself," she said, "got pictures mixed up and put the wrong names on the back. Yes, I suppose that is all there was to it." Oddly, she looked disappointed.

"And to spare the woman any embarrassment," said Uncle James, "our cousin posed for all of Levering's subsequent photographs. Beard or no beard, is there any doubt in your mind that the man who posed for this picture is the man who posed for the one Mama has upstairs in her bedroom?"

Mimi said she didn't know what to think. She went to her brother and again she looked at the picture. "I think it must be Levering," she said, "and it certainly does look like you, and me, too. But not Andrew." And then she and Uncle James began to laugh. Dear no, said Uncle James, leave Andrew out of it. This was hardly for a Philadelphia lawyer.

"Or a minister of the gospel," said Aunt Catherine, "if I may remind you. A ninety-two year old woman! I would be ashamed of myself."

"She wasn't always ninety-two," said Uncle James. "She was twenty-five when I was born."

"But, James," said Mimi, "he must have been in his sixties."

Uncle James nodded, rather proudly, it seemed to Sally. How very little one knew about people whom one had known forever.

"Honestly," said Tess, "I never heard anything so ridiculous in my life and I thought I'd heard it all when Daddy's old flame breezed in. Honestly, Mimi, you better get a television and start watching old movies."

"You may leave any time," said Mimi.

"Daddy, it isn't true that Granny had an affair with that old man, is it?" asked Tess. "I mean, Granny of all people, and a poet. Gad!"

"You see, Uncle James?" asked George.

"My eyes don't pop that much," said Tess who had captured the picture, "but I see what you mean about the mouth and chin, Jack."

"Oh, you can't really see a thing like that in an old picture," said Jack. "It was just power of suggestion. I imagine you hit on the solution, Mrs. Bradford."

"Solution, fiddle!" said Mimi. "She's been telling us for years. James, I guess you always were smarter than I. When did you catch on?"

"Say!" said Tess, "I just now remembered. She said it this afternoon. The rest of you never noticed, and I didn't think about it until now. Mimi, this afternoon she said you couldn't remember your father. She meant Adam Levering! So it's true, it really is! And none of you noticed."

"Your father just about jumped out of his shoes," said Uncle James. "Why do you think he ran home for the picture?"

"I can't understand it," said George. "I must have heard her say things like that before. One would think when I got the picture, but, no, I scarcely looked at it. I wasn't interested in Levering any more."

"But of course you are now," said Tess. She hurried over to her father's chair and squeezed in beside him. "Daddy, this will make your book a sensation. Why, it will get it out of the university libraries."

"And right into court," said Aunt Catherine. "George, I am warning you. If you dare print one word of this libel, I shall take action. I am putting it into the hands of my attorney immediately."

"Your attorney isn't going to like it," said Mimi. "I've a feeling this is a case Andrew wouldn't touch, even for a fee."

"Yes, Catherine, you would have to pay for this one," said Uncle James, and with great dignity Aunt Catherine said she was prepared to pay in her life's blood, if necessary, by which she undoubtedly meant money.

"All the same," said Mimi, "I would appreciate it if you'd delay publication until after election. George, you know what the *Courier* would do with this, in relation to my activities in the Home for Unwed Mothers."

"Oh, Mimi!" said C.J. "Not again!"

"What's the matter with you, C.J.?" asked Uncle James. "You ought to be proud of her. If more of our respectable citizens . . ."

"Respectable," said Aunt Catherine. "Don't make me laugh."

C.J. said it was just that he dreaded having Mimi go through the tiring process of campaigning only to be defeated. Mimi said she was not going to be defeated this time. "If I had known about this before," she said, "I would have tried for Washington years ago."

"No doubt," said Aunt Catherine. "And no doubt you would have got there, too, along with the other . . ."

"Dear heaven, Catherine," said Uncle James, "you nearly said something funny. Would you agree, George?"

"There is something I want you to get straight," said George as he tried to push Tess out of his chair. "I am not going to write any book on Adam Levering. When I stopped work on that manuscript, I was through with it. That is final."

"But, Daddy, you can't," said Tess. "It wouldn't be fair to

the rest of us. Oh, not just the money, darling. Look, all these years everybody thought Adam Levering didn't leave anybody and now he's got a whole slew of lovely relatives and that's history, Daddy, literary history. You can't want to keep a thing like that to yourself."

"Further dissemination of this information will not come from me," said George. "Tess, I'm going to shove you off onto the floor if you don't get out. Don't misunderstand me. I believe that Mimi and Uncle James are Levering's children, but I do not believe it can be proved. And suppose it could be? What bearing does it have on Levering's place in literature?"

"The hell with literature," said Tess. "What about us?"

"So you think every reference he made to the Church was really to Granny?" Sally asked George. "My word, it does make those hymns rather torrid."

"It was a commonplace evasion of censorship," said George. "It makes no difference who inspired the poems."

Now Tess left her father. "Oh, it makes no difference?" she asked. "Well, it makes a difference to me whether it was my great-grandmother or that old bitch Edith. I bet she wouldn't give him a divorce. Her and her lace curtains; maybe she was afraid he'd get them. I don't blame Granny a bit. I say good for her. Why not? I mean, if Edith wouldn't divorce him and if Grandfather Graham didn't do anything but play cards all the time. Oh, you all make me sick, acting like it was such a terrible thing."

"But were we, Tess?" asked Uncle James.

"Daddy and Aunt Catherine and Jack," said Tess. "Honestly!"

"You will have to resign, of course," said Aunt Catherine to Uncle James. "At least you will do me the kindness to resign before they find this out and fire you. You will never get another pulpit as long as you live. We will have to spend the rest of our days in hiding."

"Before you take to the woods, James, tell us when you first found this out," said Mimi. "I'm really very put out with you. We used to be pretty good friends."

"I nearly told you after you lost that last election," said Uncle James. "I knew it would buck you up, but on the other hand I doubted that you would believe me. I didn't have this picture, you know. And you had always had as much to go on as I'd had." He paused a moment. "But maybe you didn't. Do you suppose I got started on this track when Edith Levering slapped my face? It would be interesting to go into it with a psychoanalyst, wouldn't it?"

"You know where you'd wind up," said Aunt Catherine.

"My dear, you overwhelm me with alternatives for winding up," said Uncle James. And then he told them that he was grown, ready to enter college, before he thought about his possible connection with the old man who had lived next door. "You remember the hall back home. . . ."

Sally remembered the long hall and the wardrobe Uncle James was describing. She had stood on its seat to make faces at herself in the chipped, spotted mirror. She did not remember that Adam Levering's picture had hung there in the hall, but her mother said yes, she remembered that the picture had hung there, close to the mirror.

"Maybe I was going to a party," said Uncle James. "I don't

know why I glanced into the mirror or why, when I reached the door, I had a feeling I had seen my reflection in the glass of the picture instead of in the mirror. I went back. And something impelled me to take my hat off and hold it over the lower part of the picture. Perhaps I'd been thinking I should have shaved. I don't know if it was a sudden impulse or something that originated way back when he dandled me on his knee. All I know is that I stood there and looked into my father's eyes."

Twenty-three

CAN'T YOU REMEMBER dying wasn't all Billy ever did?" Mimi had asked Sally, but even after the rebuke, Sally had long continued to be haunted, before coming entirely awake of a morning, by a feeling that she should or could do something about her brother. This Sunday morning, watching the cat who had been alerted by the closing of the windows, she wondered why the uncomfortable thought of Billy had returned. Was it because she had unconsciously seen Billy in Tess last night? Billy, no doubt, would have been enchanted by Uncle James's claim upon Adam Levering's blood, but his malicious delight would have been directed against Granny. However, if Billy had known Jack Russak, he might have been attracted by the young doctor's vulnerability. Tess had teased Jack until he'd risen and said he had to leave to attend to his errand. He had made them all understand it would be all right with him if Tess remained with the family, but Tess had left with him.

Scowling down at the cat's meowing face, Sally wondered if the sounds in the night had really been heard last night, or if she had transferred them from other nights of listening for her daughter's return. When Tess became engaged to Jack, she refused to carry on with the house rule that obliged the children to check in with the mother. Tess said she wasn't an adolescent. Didn't her mother trust her? Repeating what she had said again and again to each of her children, Sally said it was not a matter of trust, it was a matter of wanting to know if one should call hospitals and morgues. But Tess, with her one-track mind, said at least Mother should be able to trust Jack.

Sally trusted Jack, all right, but she wondered how she would have felt if she had been Jack's mother. For Mrs. Russak's peace of mind, was it just as well she hadn't met her son's fiancée? To say nothing of the rest of the family. But what an Aunt-Catherine thought!

Tess's door, open last night when George and Sally retired, was closed now. As of course Sally had known it would be, and so why all this sighing in relief? The closed door did not mean that Tess's problem was solved, but Sally couldn't help feeling that when Tess was at home, the problem was less difficult. She had been that way about Nick, too. Nick, somehow, didn't seem so lame when he was at home.

It was six-thirty. Promptly at seven, George's internal alarm, that knew no holidays, would ring. George didn't awaken by degrees; he came immediately from deep sleep to active interest in breakfast. He wasn't the parent who had groaned when small noses pressed inquiringly close; George welcomed any extension of his day. Was it normal, Sally asked the bathroom mirror, for a person to be so damn pleased with life as George was?

When the children were too young to sleep late, Sally had longed to stay in bed until noon; when the children had to be dragged from bed, she had lost her capacity for late sleep. It had been the same way with Mimi. Mimi said she was waking up around five these days. "I read and work on my speeches," she said, "but it's all I can do to keep myself from getting up to slam doors. It must be in the blood."

It was, thought Sally as she crawled back into bed, the least harmful of the characteristics they might have inherited from the first Sarah. She thought about Dot, Scootie and Barb, and wondered if any of their graphs went back far enough to include samplings from Granny's generation. Probably not. The girls had spoken as if of a problem that had only recently arisen.

By seven o'clock she had sunk into a semi-coma from which she was roused by George's cheerful offer to bring breakfast on a tray. As he had undoubtedly known it would do, the suggestion sent his wife into her clothes. George, reared in a house where people seldom dressed for breakfast, was always impressed by the completeness of Sally's morning costumes. Impressed but perhaps sometimes exasperated? "I hadn't realized it was to be formal," he said. "Will black tie do?" Nevertheless he must have appreciated having a regular sit-down breakfast with a decently dressed companion.

"Isn't this nice?" he said when they started on their grapefruit.

He had been saying this every week since the two of them had been having Sunday breakfast alone. Sally didn't know if he meant that being alone with her was nice or if he was referring to the cherry she put on the grapefruit in honor of Sunday. She could, of course, find out by omitting the cherry, but she preferred not to take the risk.

"About last night," he said.

"Don't worry about it," she said. "Uncle James would have spilled it sooner or later. He's getting a little childish."

"Yes, when I said I should have noticed the resemblance between him and Levering . . ."

"Oh, he's not that far gone. He knew you meant more than the physical resemblance."

"But I didn't mean it as a compliment."

"You can't force him to take it as a slam."

"Old fool. How was I to know he was itching for the chance?"

Sally put two slices of bread into the toaster her mother had given George for Christmas, the machine that George still said surely was supposed to do something more than make toast. "I don't suppose it's going to kill any of us," she said. "It may even get Aunt Catherine's mind off her excretory system for a while."

"She and Jack are a pair, all right."

"Maybe we won't have to be thinking about Jack much longer," said Sally, and George said that would suit him. Would she give him the book-review section? Not that it was worth looking at. Sally said she found the section very interesting, but that was the way it went with them, wasn't it?

"I beg your pardon?" said George.

Buttering the toast, she said he and she rarely agreed on

what was interesting. "What are we going to talk about after the children have gone and it's this way all the time?"

"We could put slips in a hat," he said, "and take turns drawing. The next time we have a party, God forbid, why don't we do it? Then maybe we, too, could have a fun party. I meant to congratulate you after we left the Smiths'. You were the only woman who didn't tell Patricia it had been a fun party."

"It's just a phrase that's making the rounds, but, as I recall, you didn't contribute much to the fun."

"I couldn't remember any of the jokes until they'd got into them," he said. "What's the matter with your friends, Sally? Don't they get any sex in bed?"

When she returned with the eggs and bacon, extra bacon for George to sneak to the cat, she told him party conversation wasn't what she had wished to discuss. "What I pulled out of the hat this morning was just about us, sitting here alone," she said. "Why don't you ever talk about your business?"

"I have to talk about it five days a week. When I get home, I like to think about my own work."

"Then talk about that."

"If I talked about it, I wouldn't do it."

Without thinking she asked if doing it was so important. "Oh, I didn't mean that," she said when she noticed his hurt look. "I don't mean your books aren't important. It's just that I hate being so shut out of everything that interests you."

"It's all in there." He nodded toward the study. "But don't get things mixed up."

"Your handwriting is illegible," she said, "and your typing

isn't much better, especially after you've scrawled all over it." But then, remembering that Ann Price could make out any and all of George's papers, she went on swiftly to the published works. "You know I read everything you write, after it's published. Would you be interested in knowing that your last book has a sentence three hundred and two words long? I counted."

He was interested, but before they could go on with this subject, Tess came in. She was wearing an old bathrobe that hadn't been on the first floor in many years, but it was the absence of lipstick that told her mother there had been no reconciliation last night. "I trust you've both had enough coffee to brace you," said Tess. "Young Doctor and I have busted up."

"Well, now," said George, "that calls for more than coffee."

"I thought you'd be pleased," said Tess. "I must be psychic. But what's the matter with you, Mother? No congratulations?"

"Not until I'm asked for them," said Sally.

"At the moment I'd rather have a cup of coffee," said Tess.

"Champagne would be more suitable," said George.

"Daddy," said Tess, "you know my friend Marian. I've noticed there's nothing Marian would rather do than talk about what a heel she used to be married to, but she never seems to like it when you agree with her. Do you follow me?"

George said it was probably too subtle for him, but did she mean that the break between her and Jack wasn't final?

Tess said it was as final as Marian's divorce. Her point was there was no need to rub it in. "So I made a mistake," she said. "Can we leave it at that?"

When Sally came back with fresh coffee, George perhaps feeling unable to leave it at that, had gone to his study. Tess said it was gratifying to have been able to bring so much joy to her parents. "But why aren't you saying how much better it was to have found it out now than later?"

"I shouldn't have thought it necessary to say something so obvious," said Sally.

"From where I sit, it would have been pleasanter to find it out later."

"Then you're sitting on a cloud," said Sally. "Tess, when two people are as incompatible as you and Jack . . ."

"You'd have to go pretty far to find two people more incompatible than you and Daddy," said Tess, "and you've done all right. Oh, I didn't mean incompatible sexually."

The coffee was hot. Sally set her cup down. "Thanks."

"Look," said Tess, "if he and Mrs. Johnson hadn't been engaged so long, Aunt Laura wouldn't have had a chance to get busy with her little knife. If you hadn't married him so fast, she probably would have fixed you."

"Are you implying that somebody fixed you?"

"Damn right," said Tess. "Oh, I was keeping a sharp eye on Aunt Laura and on you, too, darling, but I sure never thought it would be Granny with her cute reminiscences."

"Jack was probably tired last night. He works hard."

"He'll always be tired; he'll always work hard. That's the way he wants it. Don't preach at me. I had enough of that last night, to the tune of a juke box. My God, what a place to break an engagement."

"I suppose you didn't do any preaching."

"I wish you'd make up your mind whose side you're on. You didn't expect me to sit there and not say a word while he traced Original Sin back to my great-grandmother, did you?" And then, without giving her mother a chance to comment, she said she was going to stay at Marian's next week. "I've got a lot of extra jobs coming up and it will save commuting."

"I don't like that woman," said Sally. "She's too old for you."

"She won't be around. She's going out of town on business."

"But, Tess, I don't want you staying all by yourself in that terrible neighborhood."

Tess said it wasn't a terrible neighborhood. Maybe it wasn't quite Gold Coast, but it wasn't quite Skid Row, either. "You're a suburban snob, dear," she said. "I wonder if it's too early to call Marian. I'd hate to wake her up."

"Especially when you undoubtedly would be waking someone else, too," said Sally.

"You sound very much like Dr. John Russak," said Tess as she filled her coffee cup again. "And right now I don't find that a very attractive way to sound."

Maybe so, thought Sally as she picked up the bacon crumbs the cat had scattered all over the carpet, but she wasn't ready to accept what Tess offered as a secondary reason for going down to Marian's. It wasn't, Tess said, that she expected Jack to come around but if he should, she thought it would be better if she weren't at home. Did she mean she thought it would be better to receive him where they could have more privacy than provided by her home or a hamburger joint? After Tess had gone, Sally went up to the girl's bedroom to look for the blue housecoat. It was a garment that would take up a lot of a small suitcase's space but, as she had suspected, it was gone.

"I'm terribly worried about Tess," she said when George finally came up to bed that night. "I don't think she's really through with Jack."

"No," said George. "I'd decided it was too good to be true."

"Marian's going to be out of town. I'm just certain Tess plans to have Jack go down there."

"Well, what do you want me to do about it?" asked George. "Go down and protect him? Let him take his chances."

"You know very well what will happen if she has her way. *Then* he'll be quick enough to want to get married."

"Seems like it used to be the other way around, in my day," said George. "I didn't know the granting of the supreme favor was supposed to make the beneficiary run for a preacher."

"We're talking about Jack Russak, not you," said Sally.

George flung his socks on the floor. "I still say there's nothing we can do. She's getting more like Nick all the time."

"Nick?"

"Yes, the Bradford's coming out."

"Bradford? It's Cutter."

"The Cutters never had that kind of determination," he said. "Anyone up against a Bradford might as well give in right away and be done with it."

"I suppose in a minute you'll be saying . . ." And then Sally was struck by an astonishing thought. "George! What exactly did you have in mind when you asked me if I'd go to California?"

"No dream so fine as the realization." He turned to bow. If he had had his pants on, his wife might have been more impressed by the speech but, without his pants, George looked and sounded very foolish.

"And all these years I've thought you acted funny because you dreaded a big wedding," said Sally. "I thought it was because you wanted us to go off to a justice. George Cutter, do you mean to stand there and say you actually thought I'd just go off!"

"Now, Mother," he said. "Where the hell are my pajamas?"

She waited until he had got into his bed. "Now," she said, "you will kindly tell me why you had the gall to think . . ."

"Sally, you know I wasn't in any position to get married."

"You and Jack Russak. Men like you are never in a position to get married. But, believe me, if I'd had any idea you weren't proposing marriage, why, you'd have got your walking papers so fast you wouldn't have known what hit you."

"I know," he said. "I think I caught on rather quickly, considering."

"Considering what?"

"Not that I really swallowed Laura's story."

"We always seem to come back to Laura." Sally propped herself up on an elbow. "I'm getting very weary of Laura."

Yes, said George, Laura was tiresome. He said maybe it would have been different if they had told her, when she was a little girl, that it was all right for her not to be as bright as the rest of them. "But we told her how well she danced, how well she spoke pieces, how well she wrote. I suppose we practically told her how well she lied. Pretending to believe her stories got to be such a habit with us that maybe we did begin to believe there was a little something in them. Oh, I never believed all the embroidering she gave your story, but I guess I did think there was some truth in it. Naturally I soon found out otherwise. Wouldn't you think she'd have had sense enough to make things simpler? She didn't have to ring May in on her story about why she and Tommy didn't get married. She could have said it was any girl. By then May and I weren't writing very often and Laura wouldn't have missed a thing like that. But no, she had to trick it up. She had to make May the girl and she had to make your paramour a relative of Capone's." He laughed. "I don't know why I believed it even for a minute, but I suppose it seemed too wild to be invented out of whole cloth."

"His relatives and the Capones were shooting each other as fast as they could," said Sally, "when I knew him, I mean. I think they made some sort of working agreement later on."

"What are you talking about?"

"Tony Cado. That's who you were talking about, isn't it?"

George said he couldn't remember if Laura had mentioned a name. His voice sounded very far away.

"You know," said Sally after she had turned off the light, "I really don't consider it any of your business, if I may quote an authority I've always considered infallible, but I wasn't Tony's mistress, if that's what she meant by paramour."

"Well," said George. He cleared his throat. "Well, I'm sure he must have been a rather nice gangster."

"Oh, he wasn't a real gangster when I was dating him," she said. "He was just sort of an apprentice. And he looked like an angel, George. And he was so serious. I can't remember ever hearing him laugh."

George asked if that hadn't got a little depressing but she said no, when people were in love they wanted to be serious. George said he understood that part of it and that he had always been very serious about love. "You?" asked Sally.

She had meant to tell him, very seriously, what she thought of people who were gay and even humorous about making love, but then she got to thinking about how he had looked when she'd told him it was short notice for a church wedding. "And to think I thought that stricken look meant you were scared of a big crowd!" she said, when she had stopped laughing enough to speak.

"That's another thing about your family," said George. "Once you people get hold of a thing, you never let go. I suppose I'll never hear the end of this." But then he began to laugh, too.

"Poor fellow," he said later on.

"Oh, I wouldn't waste any sympathy on Tony Cado," said Sally. "From what I read in the papers, he's not a very desirable citizen."

George said he wasn't thinking about Tony Cado. "I was thinking about poor old Jack," he said.

Twenty-four

SALLY HAD PERFECTED a routine for the handling of persons who solicited by phone for commercial enterprises. She was particularly skillful when the solicitors called on a Monday morning. After asking them to repeat their company's name, she would tell them she kept a list. "I never patronize places that solicit by telephone," she would say, "and especially places that hire people who haven't got sense enough to know Monday's wash day." And then she would slam the phone down and feel that the race from the basement had been worth her while.

This morning, when she was all set for the wash-day elaboration, she realized that the man who had not identified himself was poor old Jack. Jack wished to leave a message with her. Would she tell Tess to meet him at that hamburger place near the hospital at nine? He could get away then, for a few minutes, unless something came up. Sounding more like himself, he said he would send someone else over to the restaurant if it turned out he wouldn't be able to make the appointment, but that of course he would try.

"I'll give Tess the message when she calls," said Sally, "but she's going to be very busy this week and so she's staying in town." She hesitated. Tess, she knew, would call Jack if Jack didn't call her. If these two were bound to get together at least one more time, wouldn't it be better to make it appear that the idea was solely Jack's? "I don't know what her plans are for tonight, but you could call her around dinner time, at Marian's. She's staying there and . . ."

Jack said he had forgotten that Tess had planned to spend a few days at Marian's place. Perhaps some day he would become wise enough to be able to admit there could be something about which he had no prior knowledge, but he wasn't smart enough yet. Feeling uncomfortably like Cupid, Sally went down the stairs so slowly that she hadn't reached the basement before the telephone rang again. This was a man who identified himself at once. "Sally," he said, "this is Red. I just wanted to tell you how well the pictures came out."

"How nice of you," she said. "My daughter always takes a good picture, but the rest of us . . ."

"But they're good of all of you," he said. "In fact, I'm going to have a tough time deciding which to use and so I was wondering if you might drop around, if you're going to be in town anyway . . ."

She hated to say she was almost never in town. "I'm rather tied up this week," she said, "but my mother's in town every day, and I'm sure she'd appreciate the chance to help you decide."

Mr. Landis—Red, that is—said that would be splendid, but as he talked on it seemed that any of the pictures would be just dandy for the feature and that Mrs. Bradford really wouldn't have to bother. And there was no great rush, anyhow, and if Sally planned to come in town next week . . . "Tell you what," he said. "Why don't we have lunch? Yesterday I was going through some old photographs and I came across some I took when I was working on the school paper. I have a couple of you I thought you might like to see."

Considering how long it had been since she had been asked for a date, Sally thought she did rather well. She said she couldn't say, just now, what her plans for next week would be, but that she would like to see the old pictures, of course. Red made it clear that he would like to see Sally. He said he would give her a ring later on, but her old competence was returning. One wobbled a bit when one got on a bike again for the first time in many years, but the knack soon returned. She said she was going to be in and out so much that she didn't know when he would be able to catch her and so why not leave it that she would call him? This was not where Red wished to leave it, but what could he do but remind her that it was a promise? "Then I'll be expecting to hear from you in a few days," he said. And from the tone he used, Sally understood that he understood she hadn't made up her mind, and that he was willing to give a girl time to think it over. He sounded quite sure of himself.

It was difficult to go back to the washing, but Patricia was calling for her shortly before one o'clock to take her to Mrs. Abbott's luncheon in honor of Mrs. Bertram Johnson, and so Sally couldn't just sit and dream about having a beau again. There wasn't even time to speculate upon how George would feel about this, and whether it would make him wish he'd taken his wife along sometimes, instead of his precious Ann Price.

Mrs. Abbott was a woman who entertained in color. The luncheon for old May was pink, from the treacle which the hostess correctly assured her guests had next to nothing in it but syrup, to the candies that cluttered the bridge tables. The rolls were pink, the lobster sauce was pink, and the meringues, unfortunately overcooked by a hireling, were basically in the color scheme. Mrs. Johnson, in red, said she was sorry not to have toned down sufficiently.

As Patricia detoured to drive into the subdivision where the Johnsons were going to move, she remarked that Mrs. Johnson would have to tone down more than her clothes if she expected to get anywhere in Brentwood. Patricia, who had doubled the grand slam bid and made by the guest of honor, was feeling very bitter about newcomers. "A real bridge player wouldn't have taken that finesse," she told Sally. "She should have taken her one down and been content. If that finesse hadn't worked, she would have been down four."

"But she made her contract," said Sally.

"Not by playing *bridge*," said Patricia. "It was poker. Oh, she'll soon find out we don't go for that sort of thing."

However, when Sally was finally able to persuade Patricia that the grandest of the new houses bore the number Mrs. Johnson had told them, Patricia put on her glasses and after a few minutes said she might consider putting Mrs. Johnson up for membership in several organizations. "She may not be so bad, once you get used to her," said Patricia, "and that's a wonderful house for meetings. We can have outdoor things here, too. Didn't she say they have three acres? I wonder if the landscaping would be finished in time for the Flower Festival? She seems to be a very sincere sort of woman. Once you forgot about her horrible clothes and . . ."

"She's an old friend of George's," said Sally, not only because it was pleasant, for once, to be able to tell Patricia something, but because she knew that her friend would find this out eventually. "They used to be engaged."

When Patricia had finished with saying she did not believe this, she asked why Sally had always pretended that she was George's first love. She said there must have been something very strange about his engagement to that woman.

"Why, not strange at all," said Sally. "You forget he was nearly thirty when I met him. Heavens, did you think he wasn't normal? May's around his age, and it was over and done with long before I met him, and so why should I have thought to talk about it?"

"What broke it up?" asked Patricia.

"Oh, she went away for her graduate work and they drifted apart."

"She doesn't look like a drifter." Patricia stared out at the new house. "She looks like a very practical woman. I bet she met this Johnson and went into a huddle with herself. I wonder how many bathrooms it has."

Patricia was obsessed by bathrooms. Her house had only two that she felt could be counted. No, she didn't count the one on the third floor, nor did she count the powder room on the first floor or the stall in the basement. "For all practical purposes," she said, "I've only got the two bathrooms for the four of us."

"But five people can go to the toilet at one time in your house," said Sally. "I think that's terribly practical and very elegant."

Patricia said it was all right to talk like that when they were alone, but that Sally had better watch herself. "I've been wanting to tell you, dear," she said, "you're sounding more like George every day and I really think you should guard against that."

"I'm practicing up for when I come into my money and can say anything, like May Johnson," said Sally. "Darling, do you remember Red Landis? I think he was a Sigma Nu."

"Of course I remember him," said Patricia who had never yet forgotten a member of any fraternity she had considered worthy of her attention. "What about him?"

"He did the square-dance piece for the church. Uncle James was mentioning it."

"Don't you ever notice anything? His name was on the story. Clifford Landis. Poor Red, at his age."

"You mean square dancing?"

"I mean still a reporter. He might have got somewhere if he hadn't married that horrible girl. You surely remember her. She was such a mess. She belonged to one of those crumby little locals. They were engaged before they came to school. Oh, I guess she didn't come until after you dropped out. I remember he wanted us to do something about her, but she was absolutely impossible, physical ed major or something gruesome like that. You know, she went around campus in a middy blouse. Wouldn't you think that when he saw her in a different setting, he would have known she just wouldn't do? Poor Red, I always liked him. I could have got him some wonderful dates, but I guess he thought he had to be loyal to this village queen."

By now they had reached the Cutter house, but Patricia wasn't ready to stop talking. She said she was glad Sally had mentioned Red Landis. "It isn't that I don't think the world of Brad," she said, "but Red's an example of how fatal these high-school engagements can be."

"But who is engaged?"

"Darling, you can't prevent things from being by just refusing to look at them. I don't like it any more than you do. Frankly, much as I adore Brad, I don't think he's the one for Patsy."

Sally said she saw no reason for Patricia to be alarmed. "Of course I know she telephones him like mad, but it's a phase lots of girls go through . . . "

"We paid a lot for that ring," said Patricia. "I told Smitty she was too young to have such an expensive ring, but she teased him until she got it. Of course it's insured, but will he do anything when he's got a claim against a policy? I don't know why he takes out all this insurance and then won't . . . "

"What ring?"

"That emerald we gave her for Christmas. Is it possible you haven't noticed that Brad's wearing it? It's got pearls around it. She wanted diamonds, but I certainly put my foot down on that, at her age! Smitty would give her the moon, I suppose, if I didn't . . . "

"Patricia, I assure you Brad isn't wearing emeralds and pearls. Haven't you ever looked at his hands? He could no more get one of Patsy's rings on than he could fly."

"I'd rather have him wearing it than carrying it around loose," said Patricia. "Sally, if he loses that ring, I am going to raise hell. I'm warning you. And Miss Patsy is going away to boarding school next year; I don't care what Smitty says. I'll teach her to exchange an expensive ring for an old beat-up wristwatch."

"Wristwatch?"

"I suggest you ask your son what he's done with his watch," said Patricia. "Also, I suggest that you tell him Patsy is ready to return it. My God, it doesn't even run half the time."

Twenty-five

AND WHAT WAS George's considered opinion about the ring and wristwatch? Patricia, he said, must finally have heard that what would have been Billy's inheritance was being dissipated in a profit-sharing plan for the Bradford Company's employees. "I suppose she figures the daughter of such a socialist as C.J. won't have sense enough to hang on to her money long enough to make Brad a good catch. Isn't the ring insured?"

"Smitty doesn't like to put in claims," said Sally. "He doesn't want to spoil his rating."

George said it was fine to hear that the Smiths had a common interest. "If there's anything that woman's more interested in than rating . . ."

The dishes hadn't been finished yet, and Sally knew her water must be getting cold, but she had to defend Patricia. She said she didn't think it was very nice of him to talk like that about her best friend. He asked how else he could talk. "I've never yet heard you say a good word for her," he said.

How he could make such a statement! "If I criticize her

now and then, it's only in a friendly spirit," she said. "Why, Patricia's wonderful!"

"In what way?"

"She's beautiful and she's always so well dressed and . . ."

"I grant you she usually looks clean, but go on."

"She has a wonderful presence. I bet she knows more about Robert's *Rules* than any other woman in Brentwood and, believe me, if some of you men paid more attention to things like that, maybe your meetings wouldn't be such a shambles. And you know she's a marvelous hostess." Sally looked down at the dishrag in her hands. "Anyway, I've known her since we were children."

There, said George, was his answer. He picked up a manuscript and started to peruse it. Oh, hadn't she said everything? What was he going to do about Brad? "I hope you won't ask me to beat him," he said. "He's in better training than I am."

"I think it's time you had a little talk with him."

Now George finally looked alarmed. He demanded to know why his son had not been apprised of the facts of life before reaching the age of sixteen. He had been under the impression that the modern grammar school, to say nothing of the modern mother, saw to it that a child knew something about sex before . . .

"But it hasn't got anything to do with sex," said Sally. What, she wondered, would he do if she threw this rag at him?

"If it hasn't," he said, "there's something radically wrong with him and Patsy. What are they engaged for, to go into business together after they get through school?"

She said she didn't know why he had to take everything

so literally. "Patricia and I aren't afraid they'll do anything wrong," she said. "The point is that sometimes when kids get engaged in high school, it lasts and then they don't have a chance to become acquainted with other people and . . ."

"How long has the engagement lasted so far?"

"Oh, you know they aren't really engaged. That's just Patricia. She always exaggerates everything. I wouldn't say they're even going steady, just because they traded something for a couple of days. Brad isn't interested in girls yet. Why, he's only sixteen and boys are always at least two years behind girls."

George looked at his manuscript again. "Well, I'll be glad to speak with Patricia, next time I see her. Yes, indeed, very glad."

When Sally had interrupted her dishwashing to come to the study, she hadn't planned to mention Red Landis, but George's proposal to have a talk with Patricia made her so angry that she decided now was a good time to tell him about her telephone call. After making him promise never to mention the ring and watch to Patricia and thereby endanger a lifelong friendship, she asked if he would mind if she had lunch with another man. He said no, not if she didn't have to pay for the meal.

"I wish you would be serious for once," she said. "That *Courier* reporter wants me to have lunch with him."

"Didn't he get enough for his story?"

"The invitation seemed to be social."

"I'll be darned." He put the manuscript down. "I would have said he was more interested in Tess."

"George, I don't mean the boy! The reporter, not the photographer."

"The old duck?"

"He and I were in school together."

"Then he must have been very retarded. I don't know why you'd want to have lunch with an old geezer like that."

"You have lunch with other women."

"God, yes. You know what we had today? For the main course, mind you. A plate of fresh fruit, all very green, with a cream puff in the middle. And you know what was inside that cream puff? Raspberry ice."

"Doesn't Ann let you do your own ordering?"

"It was a party she arranged for the woman who does our handcraft series. I never did like that woman but, by God, when she poured French dressing on that raspberry ice . . ."

"George, the thing is that I do like Red. I think he's very attractive."

"Red?"

"Mr. Landis."

George said Whitey would be a better nickname for the old geezer. He said he thought Uncle James was far more attractive than Mr. Landis, and so why didn't she have lunch with her uncle, instead?

"Yes," she said, "when it hits home, you aren't so sure you favor the single standard, are you? Well, I'm sorry, but maybe I've listened to you too long to make a sudden switch." And off she went to the kitchen, but he yelled after her.

"If you're thinking of more than lunch," he yelled, "why bother with substitutes? Why not get in touch with Tony Cado?"

She whirled around, hurried back into the study and closed

the door. "George!" she said. "For heaven's sake! Brad's at home."

He got up and slung the cover at his typewriter. "Then let's clear out of here," he said. "Let's take a walk and end up at Tess's hamburger joint. I can still taste that damned sherbet."

And his unusual mood continued while they walked along the shore of the placid lake. He wasn't fooled by the balmy evening. "You just see," he said. "We aren't through shoveling snow."

And when had he done any shoveling? But Sally spoke of Florida and of how soon it would be when Brad went away to college. "Why don't you quit your job then? You know C.J.'s always said I can have part of my money any time."

"Quit my job!"

"But, darling, you're going to have to quit some time and wouldn't you like to give all your time to your own writing?"

Eventually, said George, but he certainly wasn't going to go off and sit on his backsides in Florida as long as he could still make it to the office. Sixty-five? Well, he and Ann were working on a revision for the retirement plan, so that the company would be able to retain an employee if it appeared to be to the mutual advantage. Under the new plan, there would be financial provision for those who wished to retire at sixty-five or even sooner. It was going to be a much more sensible arrangement.

As he spoke of the new plan, he returned to his usual good humor and to his habit of walking a few paces ahead of his wife. It wasn't long before he worked up an appetite. Yes, he knew it was early and dinner had been fine, but he could do with a hamburger now. However, in the restaurant he wasn't too sure. Did Sally think the place smelled of horse meat?

"That's just burned fat from the French fries," she said. "Horse meat smells sort of sweet. I know because I cooked some for the cat when he wouldn't eat it raw. He wouldn't eat it cooked, either."

"Not having the cat along," said George to the waitress, "we'll have ham on rye."

"No sandwich for me," said Sally. "Just coffee."

"I suppose not having the cat along, you wouldn't want a glass of milk?" the waitress asked George.

"You started it," said Sally, after the bright waitress had left, but George was scowling at the juke-box gadget and asking if people actually put dimes in these things nowadays. He said he bet Sally's friend Cado was mixed up in this racket and when she said no, that Tony was mixed up in slot machines, he said it was the same thing.

"George," she said while she waited for her coffee to cool, "what would you do if something happened to me? I mean, if I died."

"I would die, too."

"Don't be silly."

"Then don't ask silly questions."

"People who have been happily married always get married again."

He said he did not intend to get married again. "What's that stuff in the jar?"

"Mustard. But you didn't intend to get married in the first place, did you? I keep forgetting."

"It certainly doesn't look like mustard."

"It's the fluorescent light," she said. "It makes everything look ghastly."

"Not you," he said. "You look fine. Do you suppose it's safe?"

"Of course it's safe. This is where all the hospital people eat."

"Before going in?" He sniffed at the jar. "It doesn't smell like mustard."

"Mustard doesn't smell, anyway not enough to smell it in here. You would get married so fast. I suppose for the children's sake you'd wait a decent interval but then you'd marry . . . " She drew back from the rim of the dark chasm. She did not say Ann Price's name. ". . . you would marry some young chit."

"I don't know why people always say *young* chit," he said. "Chits are not chits unless they are young, but you picked out my first wife and I absolutely insist upon picking out the next one. I wonder if I could persuade that girl to reconsider. You know the one I mean, the one who always vanted to be alone. Whatever happened to her?" He took a bite of his sandwich and announced that the paste did not taste like mustard. "What about you? It's far more likely that I'll die first. I wonder if this stuff is poison. There's no label."

"One thing sure," said Sally, "I do not ever intend to have another husband."

"Poor Tony, poor Whitey," said George as he carefully scraped the mustard from the ham. "What was it you told me Tess said? I don't know how she could say we're incompatible."

"I told you she amended it. She said she didn't mean sexually."

George studied his sandwich and then pushed it away. "You know," he said, "I don't think that's ham. She said what?"

"You heard me."

"I never thought about it before," he said, "but maybe you should have taken some of your money a long time ago. Maybe our house is too damned small."

Twenty-six

RUSHING AROUND ON the second floor of her in-laws' house, Sally pinned and sewed, and wished she had come early enough to wash and iron. "Suppose they didn't have you," Mimi had said, "would they go hungry and naked?"

Sally hadn't had time, really, to stop by to see her mother late this afternoon, but she had wanted to deliver the news personally. "We still have to work out a few details," Tess had said when she telephoned this noon, "such as will I keep on with my job, but we've agreed on everything that matters." But Sally and Mimi, hiding from the ruler of the Bradford house, agreed on nothing. If they had waited until they had rested, they would have had better sense than to think either of them could call Tess's wedding tune.

Sally had had a hard day at the art school where she had acted as messenger and buffer between Helen and the janitor. Mimi's day in town must have been a difficult one, too, because in addition to being stubborn about weddings, she was caustic about the catering and maid service Sally supplied Rita and the Cutter girls. "How do you suppose they ever got along before you took over?" she asked. "Sally, you're getting more like your grandmother every day. Can't you relax?"

And what happened last year when Sally relaxed her vigilance long enough to let Rita finish her own dressing? How Rita laughed when her attention was called to the garters and safety-pins gleaming through the lace of her dress. "But then what did I do with my slip?" she asked. The slip was discovered, eventually, under her bed pillow, along with a box of what she had assumed were chocolates, but which turned out to be the needles and thread her daughter-in-law had been hunting. "Mercy," Rita had said, "what with creating a sensation at the show and coming home to that box, I would have been quite stuck up." Then, looking very pleased with herself, she had said she guessed she could hold her own with the Cutter men.

"I can't keep them from saying ridiculous things," Sally told her mother, "but at least I can try to keep them from looking like freaks."

However, when she regarded her own and Rita's reflections in her mother-in-law's bedroom mirror, Sally wondered if there was something cheap about her new dress. It had not been cheap in price, and she could find no justification for the extravagance. If she had felt the need of change, why hadn't she bought new accessories for her perfectly good black dinner dress? Cézanne blue, the elegant clerk had said of this taffeta that reminded Sally a little of her daughter's housecoat. She felt very conspicuous when she took off her work smock, but her in-laws had confined their remarks to the meal. Rita and Helen said they had never tasted anything so good. Laura, after stating that she didn't particularly like stew, admitted that tonight's had been edible. Perhaps the new dress wasn't so dramatic as Sally had thought. One thing sure, it lacked the patina the years had given Rita's pink georgette.

Twisting a pulled thread into a black dot, Rita murmured names she associated with the days when her dress had been pinker. They were names rarely heard outside of classrooms or libraries, but Sally had learned to look impressed by their mention. "Everyone came here," said Rita, "from all over the world. We had such an interesting life." Then, as if fearing she had put a blight upon the younger woman, she quickly added that they still had a wonderful time. "And it's better to be more moderate about it. We were too satisfied, before. I'm so glad you got George away from us before it was too late for him. I wonder if the girls might still get married if I went into an old ladies' home. I must ask your uncle if you have to be religious to get into all of those places. He might know of one that's more broad-minded."

"Please hold still." Sally pinned a collection of dingy straps to a shoulder seam. "We don't want to have to traipse all over the country to see you. I won't pin the other side till we get there and have your corsage."

Rita brightened. Had her wonderful boy? Indeed he had, said Sally. The corsages had been delivered to the school this afternoon and she had put the boxes in a safe, cool place. And among the instructions for Brad and George in the note left on the kitchen table had written: "George, don't look stupid if they thank you for flowers."

"I can't get over what all you've done for him," said Rita.

"He never used to be thoughtful. Don't you ever dare tell May, but I used to send flowers to her. I was good at forging, before my fingers got stiff, and it saved the Professor the nuisance. Banks aren't nearly so smart as they let on. We only had trouble once, but the Professor fixed it by telling them he'd been drinking. . . . I should have told George what color to get."

"I imagine he ordered those little pink roses you're so fond of."

"I used to get quite a lot of flowers. Really. There was one man especially. . . . Of course it didn't mean anything—he was French, but I enjoyed it. I suppose you think I'm foolish. You're so sensible and of course that's the best way."

"Do you mind if I tie your hair ribbon again?"

"It isn't quite the right shade, is it? But nobody will notice on a galloping horse, as my mother would say. The Professor didn't like M. Gilbert, but I'm sure it was for academic reasons."

Sally laughed. "Yes, men can be very academic about such things."

"The Cutter men never were very demonstrative, but you get so you know. My, how I miss the Professor. Why do women keep on marrying older men when they know they're almost sure to outlive them? I don't understand it. Nature is usually so clever. You'd think it wouldn't go to the bother of making us last so long after there's no use for us any more."

Sally stepped back to study the retied ribbon. "There, now, you look beautiful. In the Lincoln Park zoo when they can't think of anything good to say about an animal they put 'Aids balance of nature' on the sign. Maybe that's what we're supposed to do after we're through bearing and rearing children. Maybe the reason we have trouble trying to figure out what we're good for is because we don't co-operate with nature like the lower animals do. We always think we have a better idea."

"You young people are so much smarter than we ever were," said Rita. "But I still think I'd rather be human. That's what I couldn't bear about the Presbyterians. Did I ever tell you I went to Presbyterian Sunday School for a while when I was a child? I don't remember ever resigning. Maybe the Presbyterians would take me in one of their homes if I'd promise not to say anything against predestination."

Sally said she couldn't stand around talking nonsense, she had to see how Helen was coming along.

"Yes," said Rita, "the poor child's always so frightened just before a show opens."

But the artist seemed more angry than frightened. Several months ago, when searching for mobile material, Helen had discovered a fiesta costume in an old trunk she hadn't entirely unpacked when she had returned from Mexico. It was a white, flounced gown heavily embroidered in large multicolored flowers and it was, of course, too short. Sally knew there was nothing she could do to prevent Helen from wearing the dress, but she had decided to try to rule out the mantilla.

Helen had fastened Rita's Spanish comb on with shoe strings knotted under her chin. The mantilla hid the strings but, she said, she had made the fatal mistake of washing her hair. "I wanted to pep the tint up, but now my hair's so damn slippery that every time I crack a smile, the walls come tumbling down." She spread her lips into a skull's grimace and the comb and lace tilted. "Fix it, Sal."

"It seems a pity to cover your hair, after you went to all that work. Did you notice how it matches some of the flowers?"

Helen said she had got a pretty good do on her hair this time. "I don't know why I should wear the contraption if I don't want to, do you?"

"No Mexicans coming."

Going to peer out of a window, Helen said she wondered if anyone would come. "The paper said snow."

"Oh, well," said Sally. "They're hardly ever right."

"I wish I'd thought of it sooner. Do you think your father has enough of an in with the *Courier* to make that bitch write my show up?"

"I doubt it." And suppose Helen knew Sally had muffed a possible chance at an in with the *Courier*? "I shouldn't think you'd want her to come out. You know she's never said anything good about your work."

"Who cares, so long as she says something?" Helen took a cigarette from the pack Sally had given her at dinner. "I have something to sell, but how am I going to sell it if people don't know it's on the market? Break it down and is it so much different from washing machines? Oh, I'm glad you like the new show and all that, but try to look at it the way your father would."

"Are you sure you'd want me to?" said Sally before she left to see how Laura was progressing. "He took the Art Institute out of his will when they put the *Song of the Lark* in the basement."

She hesitated a moment at Laura's door. She was going to have words with Laura. "You changed your mind about going," she said, to warn her sister-in-law that the interview was to be unpleasant.

"Oh, no," said Laura. "I'm just putting on my formal for a quiet evening at home." She went to her dressing table and started to comb her hair.

Sally sat down on the crumpled bed. "May's husband got here yesterday. May Tabor Johnson's husband."

"How too thrilling."

"She's bringing him tonight."

"She wouldn't miss a chance like that."

"The thing is, will you? I think we're going to have a very successful party, providing you behave."

"*Provided,* dear. But aren't you talking to the wrong person?"

"Yes, I suppose I should have taken it up with George, too. He's not going to like it if you say anything that casts reflection on May, and he might get rather noisy."

"George, noisy?" Laura smiled into the mirror. "Dear, I think he's recovered from May by now."

"He knows a good deal, Laura. I don't know nearly as much, but even I know a lot."

Laura finished pinning her braids across the top of her head before she said she wondered. "I really wonder if you do. Hand me those slippers. Sally, it's amazing how you can insulate yourself. I quite envy you."

Sally handed the tarnished silver slippers over. "I know you do," she said. "I'm sorry, but there's nothing I can do about it. He's your brother, and you can't have it any other way."

"Well, really!" Laura bent over to put on her slippers. When she straightened up she said she supposed she shouldn't mind anything Sally said. "If it helps you to keep on being so blind, go ahead."

"I'm glad you mentioned that," said Sally. "Because Ann will be there tonight, too, and she's another person I don't want insulted. Ann's a very good friend of ours, Laura."

"I know she's a very good friend of George's." Laura went to the closet for a black silk jacket that had once belonged to a suit Rita had worn to funerals. "I started with the company eight years ago and the friendship was very well established even then. Everybody knew. I will say for Ann that she's never been underhanded about it."

It was easier, for a moment, to speak of clothes. "If you have to wear a jacket, why not the Chinese one?" What bothered Sally most, she decided, was Laura's superior manner. The kind of relationship that existed between George and Ann was such an old question that it was beginning to lose its power to disturb George's wife. "Black is terrible with that gray."

"Anything to please you." Laura exchanged jackets. "I'm sorry, but surely you must know she's scheming to get him away from you."

"But hasn't she been rather slow?"

"You poor little thing." Laura took some pins from the dresser and began to place them between the frogs of the jacket so there would be no possibility of anyone's getting a peek at her décolletage. "Don't you realize what your only hold has been? She isn't completely depraved, I suppose. She's waiting until the children are old enough not to be hurt by the divorce—if you can call it waiting. But the minute Brad leaves for college . . ."

"Then I've got a year or so to sharpen up. You'll have to help me. A woman who has been married to the same man as long as I have gets into sort of a rut. What do you think I should do? Dye my hair and start running around with other men?" Sally got up. "Do you have a handkerchief? Come on. Helen and Rita have gone down."

"I suppose you think you're being terribly clever."

"No, dear, just devious. Which reminds me, I wanted to tell you I wasn't Tony Cado's mistress. Or do you think 'moll' would be a better word, since he was a gangster? But wasn't he just about the handsomest boy you ever saw?"

When Laura said she had no idea who Tony Cado might be, Sally gave her a little push toward the hall. "Oh, Laura, don't be such an old stick! You know you were mad about him. All the girls were. Some time I'll have to tell you how Patricia nearly broke her neck trying to get a date with him."

"I'm glad you can be so gay."

"Yes, we're coming," called Sally and then she turned back to Laura and said perhaps it would be better to be direct. "Since you don't care for the devious, maybe I should tell it to you straight. One more false move out of you and you're going to be among the unemployed. And don't think I can't get you fired. Next time you go gunning for May or Ann or me, you just stop and consider what your chances would be for a job in an office where your brother isn't the boss. Rita's income stops with her and Helen doesn't make enough to support the two of you. Think it over."

"For cry-eye, step on it!" screamed Helen and when they reached the lower hall she told them it had started to snow. "For days and days we have spring," she said. "Little flowers begin to bloom, birds make nests and then Cutter has a preview and what happens? The biggest damn blizzard in recorded history!"

Twenty-seven

BUT, AS GEORGE pointed out when he got into the car, it wasn't snowing very hard, yet. And where was Brad? Well, Patricia had telephoned just before dinner to ask Brad to come over and eat with them. "He was in the tub and so I had the pleasure of chatting with her," said George. "Seems when she got home and found the maid baking Brad's favorite cake . . . "

"You mean Patsy, don't you?" asked Sally. "You said Patricia."

"It was Senior, herself," said George. "Maybe C.J.'s made a killing we haven't heard about."

Sally said he could be sure there was something they hadn't heard about. "Cake, my hat! How does she know what he likes? I bet he hasn't asked Patsy for the spring dance. I never could trust that woman. Did he wear his overshoes?"

"Why don't we move some place where we won't have to wear clothes?" asked Helen.

"Now, dear," said Rita, "it's just because you haven't got started on something new yet. Your father was always at loose ends between books."

"That's a state his son's never in," said Sally. "George gets going on something new before he's finished the old."

"You see, Helen?" said Rita. "If you'd do like your brother, you wouldn't have these periods of depression. And Laura always has something on the fire, don't you, Laura? My goodness, there's too much going on for us to go off to the tropics. Where do you think we should go?"

The increasingly poor visibility forced Sally to concentrate upon her driving, and so she didn't bother to correct any of the mistakes that were made before they reached the art school. These Cutters were almost as weak in geography as they were in mathematics. "Cover your heads," she said when she discharged her passengers, "or you won't any of you live to climb coconut trees. George, I don't know why you didn't wear a hat. There's no charge for checking."

"Now, Mother, don't be nervous," he said. "They'll come. The snow didn't start early enough to keep them away."

But it had started early enough to make Sally careful not to get too close to the curb. The car ahead of her might have some trouble later on. Parked by some man, she bet. And, sure enough, there he was. It was Dr. Russak. "But where's Tess?" Sally called to him. "I thought you were going to pick her up at Marian's."

"I let her out at the door," said Jack with just enough reproof in his voice to force Sally to mention that George's mother had difficulty with stairs. She did not add that Helen and Laura, both able-bodied, were capable of assisting their mother or that when George parked a car, a ticket was the least of the many things that could happen. Anyway, it seemed better to speak of the wedding before they reached lights.

"Tess tells me you're planning a June wedding," she said as they hurried along together.

"Yes," said Jack. "I've finally managed to work it so I'll have a week's vacation before going in with Dr. King."

Tess hadn't said anything about Dr. King. "How wonderful!" said Sally. "I didn't know that was definite."

"Mrs. Cutter," he said, "I could hardly be getting married so soon if I didn't see my way clear."

"It won't be long now before you're going to have to call me something else," she said. " 'Mother' shouldn't be too hard for you. George calls me that half the time, but if you'd rather use our first names, it would be all right."

"Thank you," said Jack. "That's very kind."

He would call them "You" for several years, she thought when they went up the short flight of stairs to the first floor, but eventually his children would help him ease into something else. She wondered how George would like it when Jack started calling him Gramps or some such, but at the moment George was behaving himself. He shook hands and said he had had the splendid news that he was soon to be rid of Tess. Then Helen, who at the sight of Jack had started bellowing the wedding march, kissed the doctor.

"Well, kid," she said to Tess, "it wasn't easy, but we finally dood it."

Before the corsages had all been pinned on, Sally's parents and grandmother arrived. After Granny had been persuaded to give her sealskin into the keeping of the total stranger who was manning the checkroom, she demanded to know whose wedding they were talking about. "Mine," said Tess. "Isn't it wonderful?"

"You silly thing," said Granny. "Next, I suppose you'll be wanting to borry my lace collar."

Sally tried to catch her daughter's eye to warn her not to make a fuss, but Tess was beaming. "Darling, could I?" she asked. "And could I wear Mr. Levering's pin, for something blue?"

"Whose pin?" asked Granny.

"Your cameo." Tess pointed to the pin. "The one Mr. Levering gave you."

Granny touched the cameo. "Mr. Levering? Why, that man never give anybody the time of day. He was near, Mr. Levering was. Mr. Graham give me this pin to match my eyes. It don't match yours."

"No, hers are more the color of Cousin Henry's," said George.

"A lot you know about Cousin Henry," said Granny. "He was butchered at Shiloh before you was born."

"But, Mama," said Mimi, "I thought Cousin Henry was killed by the Indians."

"Oh, you and your brother and your Indians," said Granny. "Where's James at? Wouldn't that woman leave him come?"

C.J. told her it was still early. "They'll be here directly. Why don't we take a turn around the gallery before it gets crowded?"

"First," said Helen, "I'd like to explain that this is an autobiographical sequence."

"We have programs," said Laura. "We can read."

"So if you look at Number One first," said Helen, "and then follow the numbers consecutively, I'm sure when you've seen the whole works you'll know more about me than I know myself. Sally, where the hell's the janitor?"

"Sally, come here," said Granny. "Your sash has got all whopperjawed so's the bow is off to the side."

"But it's supposed to be on the side," said Sally and at last got compliments on the dress. George asked if it was new.

"I showed it to you," she said.

"But it looked different on a hanger," said George and when C.J. said yes, it would, even Jack smiled.

"You just can't beat blue taffeta," said Tess and, thought Sally, openly leered.

"She was wearing blue the first time I ever saw her," said George.

"Brown," said Laura. "I distinctly remember because it was such an odd shade and trimmed in a sort of orange."

While his sister went on with revolting details which would have convinced most people that Laura Cutter had a photographic memory that could not be questioned, George winked at his wife. "It was blue," he said, "blue with a sort of thingamajig around the neck."

"Why, yes," said Mimi, "I remember that dress. I remember we played hookey from Miss Vance and went to a shop."

And Sally, too, remembered the dress she wore the first time she went to the Cutters' house. It was a green print Miss Vance had recommended as being "mixy" enough not to show anything. And, trailing her aloof escort that night, had Sally wondered if the print had failed to show enough?

But this was superimposing later wisdom upon memory. However, why not? What was the value of memory if it had to remain static?

Sally bowed a little to her sister-in-law's skill at inventing a costume more unflattering than the actual one had been but, absolutely certain of at least one of her maternal grandparents, she did not kowtow. "Yes," she said, "I was wearing blue that night. I always knew it was my best color. And don't you remember, Laura? You'd told me your brother was dying to meet me."

As they went into the first of the exhibit rooms, she was thinking how unfair it was for Helen to be saddled with Laura for the rest of her days. Perhaps, later on, they could hit upon a more equitable division of the burden so that Helen might sometimes go off to warm sands. But there was no need to worry too much about Helen. When Sally made the rounds of the show this afternoon, she was very aware of the kinship between George and Helen. They were vigorous individuals, and it made no difference whether the society in which they lived understood or admired them; they would always command respect and even awe.

Uncle James must have caught something of this impression when he and Aunt Catherine joined them as they stood in front of the painting titled *Conception.* The minister spoke of eternal verities, of Old Masters and of stained glass. Aunt Catherine said it was a technical trick, but she was interrupted by her mother-in-law.

"James, that's the pattrun we had down home," said Granny of the canvas that was covered with a formal design of sex symbols. "Sally, ask that woman where she got it. I always did think it was the prettiest linoleum I ever seen. Mr. Levering used to admire it so much when he'd be setting there in my kitchen."

"I don't remember him in the kitchen," said Uncle James. "He used to sit in the parlor."

"In my parlor! Do you think I'd let him stink up my good lace curtains?" asked Granny. "James, you never did remember anything straight, but I'd think you could recollect him a-writing there on my kitchen table. That's where he wrote his essay on Thanksgiving."

"See here!" said George but, saying she wanted his opinion of a smaller picture, Sally pulled him away from the group.

"I'm not going to put up with any of your wisecracking tonight," she said when she'd got him off to a corner.

"Wisecracking!" said George. "That Thanksgiving essay is one of the few dated manuscripts that have survived. It was not written on Granny's or anybody else's kitchen table. Levering wrote it while he was still away at war."

"Oh, sure, it's all right, it's hilarious when she breaks our hearts by snatching him away from us just when we'd got used to the idea he was ours," said Sally, "but let her contradict something *you* think is true and . . ."

"I have a photostatic copy of that manuscript."

"And what about us being photostatic copies?"

"Sally, your sole witness is unreliable. She doesn't even stay on the same side." He frowned at the painting that bore a piece of real rope. "Did Jack tell you he's condescended to give Doc King a whirl? Maybe you were wrong about Tess being up to monkeyshines."

"The business about Granny must have unhinged me," said Sally. "Of course now that I know the whole thing was a myth . . ."

"I did not say that I discredit the evidence of that photograph."

"But, as you said, it isn't evidence that would stand up in a court of law. Anyway, didn't you just now hear her say Cousin Henry was in the Civil War?"

"I heard her say he was butchered at Shiloh. You may recall that my old picture is of a man home from war."

"The woman who wrote that may have been the sweetheart of a whole regiment. Probably she couldn't remember which was which. People look alike in uniforms."

"If that's the way you want it," said George. "I still can't see any dog in this painting, but maybe it's because I haven't the feminine mind. What's the racket?"

Sally looked toward the hall. People were beginning to come. It must have been snowing heavily now because they were stamping their feet, shaking their coats and using the loud, exhilarated voices of persons who have momentarily bested the elements. "Let me fix your hair," she said.

"I've been going to that barber for twenty years," George said as he bent over, "but here lately he always seems to miss a piece."

She draped the long lock over the thinning spot he evidently didn't know he had. "There, now, if you'll just leave it alone . . . "

"I'm prettier than Whitey, don't you think? Anyway taller. When is it you're having lunch with him?"

"We didn't make it definite. I said I'd call him some time." Then, noticing how smug George's smile was, she added that he better not be too sure she would never make the call. "Come on, I think we should get the old ladies settled in the next room before that mob comes in here."

"Land, yes," said Granny, when Sally suggested they go where there were chairs. "You don't want to keep Mrs. Cutter standing, all crippled up." She took Rita's arm. "You poor old soul, have you had your second stroke yet?"

No, said Rita, she had had only the one.

"Well, then," said Granny, "you got no call to look so peaked. The third's what you have to watch out for. Was you a man, you'd have a right to fret. Yes, many's the man I've saw took by his second, but it's different for a woman."